The Future of My Story

J. Marlbor Alvarado

Cover and interior layout by Blue Pen

ISBN: 978-0-578-87577-4

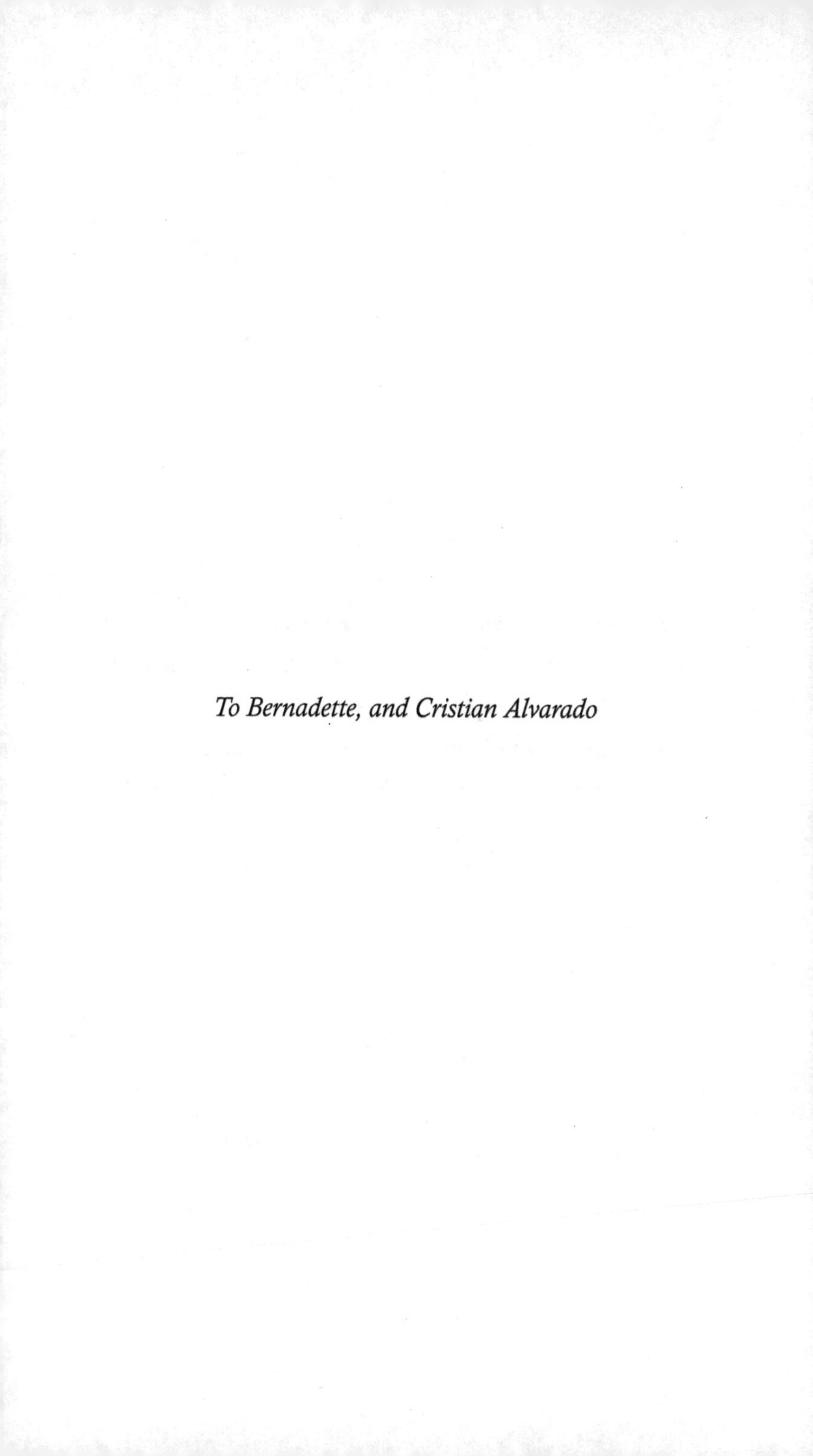

To Bernadette, and Cristian Alvarado

If joy is down a road, you don't stop to see if there are footprints left by other walkers before moving forward. An open and deep mind will show you
a road that leads beyond your simple reality to a place that might make you even happier. Live how you want once again!

It is a valley adorned with rocks, sand, and grass, seated in the northeast of Staten Island, New York, where the Verrazano-Narrows Bridge offers another and spectacular entrance to the United States of America. Some tips hang from trees, touch the grass, and barely reveal a single human loneliness. And he—that lonely life that serves as a theme here—is an old man who suffers from pain but enjoys the sound that only silence and distance allow him to notice. He has the qualities of a straight man and is delicate and reserved, although this does not coincide with his way of dressing. He wears a white shirt, fine linen but wrinkled, which he makes up for with elegance, and his pants are khakis, the fabric of which are exquisite but scruffy and pursed. On his feet are strong shoes made of old rawhide– Greek classics, but in a quarter size.

He does not find happiness but neither does he seem to be looking for it. He believes such a state of being cannot surprise anyone and can be found anywhere. And so he shifts slowly and thoughtfully. He strokes his silver beard and fixes his gaze to nothingness, trying to find the bottom of the wind. Slowly, he stretches his hand and grips an old white cup made from porcelain of the legendary French brand Le Sévre from the old but strong table that is made from red oak. He always keeps his perfect spot in front of the house, steeps, and drinks.

Assembled in sadness, the old man laughs. He seems lost in his mind and does not understand the meaning of life. But he takes a breath—a deep breath that matches the deep attention he has placed on the space ahead of him. With an expression of grief, he closes his eyes, smiles, then opens them. He looks at the sky, at the clouds, at the trees, and also the herbage, then picks up the cup of hot tea in his hand. He places it back on the small table, looks at his hands and his palms, then he raises his arms, as if trying to feel and caress the concave wind that emerges to happily lick the figs and flowers that surround him. And so he stays for a good while; perhaps he found in the silence of the space an opportunity to appreciate what to us, many times, is unknown.

With a subtle twist of the face, he turns back and also around. He takes a newspaper from the little table and moves toward the front of the house. There he sits, crosses his legs, and opens the morning paper. From time to time, he mumbles about what he reads; he also comments aloud. The man closes his worn eyelashes in search of another second of concentration, then opens his eyes, and with all the calm that his abated body allows, he places the newspaper back on the small table, gets up from the chair, and there he stays— completely anchored between the pavement and the horizon. He looks toward that muddy space in distant dreams that served so many round trips. He also sees the aged paths of many dreamers and few modern slaves to which the routine has condemned the so-called peoples' society. The old man is frozen, as if his eyes collided with his own consciousness, lost in an inaccurate world. But he is revived, and now he walks around the house.

As he advances, he observes every corner of that place and everything his eyes let him see. He reaches the bottom of the courtyard and stops and stands in front of a grave that is before him; he is sad then. He approaches it and moves his hand as if to dust off that beautiful cross made of Belgian black marble, but stops and does not. He turns around and enters the house, crosses the room, and arrives at his bedroom, opens the doors of the closet and from one of the darkened corners, pulls out an old suitcase. It seems he went a long time without taking it out or opening it, and trying to do so gives him a hard time, but he does; the little dust on it jumps, and he coughs. There are some old letters and photographs; his face reflects traces of the memories. He smiles and grieves as he takes the things and examines them. He is calm and takes time to enjoy, with joy or melancholy, the road that loneliness has taken him.

"Time passes by, and my skull becomes smoky," he mumbles.

He has discovered that his life and his green roads have always been there, at his mercy. He wants to see those always fringed fields. He does not have to suffer from such pervasive silence; in truth, he is surrounded by the aromatic vapor of free songs and does not want to suffer the cold. He is a soul that has a strange life, but real nature has compensated him.

The name of this place may not matter so much, but it is a lavish terrain, similar to the area where the old man lives, but where the minute and hour are debated head-to-head and the heat of the summer seems capable of stifling a disoriented winter and warms its cold. Absent is the magic of autumn with the ability to wither the most splendid of its flowers.

He gets out of bed and takes a shower. Paquito is his name, and at just twenty years old, he already shoulders the responsibilities of an adult man. He is Mrs. Rosa's only child and faithful to his obligations, with a good job, so far a good education, but also and more importantly, a lot of goals for the future. Of Hispanic Jewish descendent, the young Quisqueyan ("Quisqueya" was the name given to the island of the Hispaniola by the Taínos before Christopher Columbus arrived in 1492 and the Friar Dominicans who called it "La Hispaniola") is difficult to distinguish; he is light skinned, and his hair is of amber color and wavy. His nose is finelined as any of his origin, and his chocolate brown eyes similarly reveal his Indo-European descent.

He brushes his teeth, makes his habitual gargle, then washes his face. What a relief he feels as the warm water is dumped over his face. Again and again, he does this, and with his fingertips, he squeezes the corners of his eyes to get rid of those nasty eye boogers that bother him so much. It is a divine sensation to live faithfully every day, to go to work, to socialize with, whether you like it or not, those many who dislike you but also with those with whom you have a good relationship. Whether they suit you or don't suit you, different or similar people, this is normal in any modern society of "give and take."

After finishing with a simple and practical breakfast, he says goodbye to his mother, Mrs. Rosa de Dauhajre, a very energized forty-eight- year-old woman of medium height. Her hair could be easily confused with that of her son because of the similarity between them—both amber in color and curly. She is undoubtedly a very dedicated mother to her son. Mrs. Rosa twists quickly and picks the dishes from the table while Paquito leaves the apartment and, once again, encounters the same scenarios he always does in those first hours of the weekdays: a well-dressed neighbor rushing out of his house because he is running late for work; a merchant who no longer attracts attention with the noisy gate of his cellar every time he opens it, because his day always begins this way, and he has to look for sustenance for his family; some trucks and vans, which are parked to unload and supply the area's businesses with products; and a few more people, who, along with Paquito, walk in the same manner and then take the train that will take them to their respective job sites.

The morning is beautiful in that colonial city of tropical air. But the romanticism of those first hours of the day go unnoticed by Paquito, who focuses on shifting his plans for opportunities and achievements the new day will bring him. He arrives at the station, where he takes the corresponding train. As always, he sits down and opens a book, which he regularly carries with him to read, to relax, but, more than anything, to motivate himself and be successful in life.

It is his daily routine to go to work, return home after spending at least nine hours outside, have dinner—usually something light that his mother prepares that will not feel heavy at that time of night—and then sit in a beautiful rattan chair in the corner of his room and entertain himself by doing one of his favorite pastimes: painting.

It once again reaches a new morning, and as usual, Paquito commences with all the things he does upon waking up: goes straight to the bathtub, brushes his teeth, does his gargling, dresses, and has breakfast. He then leaves the place, takes the subway, opens his book, and reads. There are a lot of people on the subway, not that that surprises him. He, just like most of them, would adapt to the boring day-to-day that life had provided them.

Could it be that we are destined to live like robots in this life?

It is what comes to the mind of young Paquito as he watches discreetly but curiously the attitudes and postures that other passengers exhibit. He wants to do something different. He thinks about it, but he does not really believe he could be the object of any divine vision or the subject of the romantic theory that a ray of light could come down from the sky and predestinate that he had been chosen by the highest power for a special mission. He retires the book, and looks outside to the outskirts of town; he sees buildings, some residences, some empty lots, and the impressive Verrazano-Narrows Bridge emerging from its foggy surroundings and rising over bushes and trees. But it is something in particular that catches his full attention; there, in the distance, he sees a man sitting on a hill in the middle of empty grassland. It is during one of those untimely stops that subways make when he observes, so slightly and only for that short moment, a simple scene but one that would remain in his mind for a long time. At this moment, Paquito cannot understand the consequential nature of this sighting.

Normally, Paquito thinks, *you see men like this—homeless, poorly dressed, and bearded—snooping, screaming, begging for tips or something to eat, complaining, bothering everyone around them. But this man, despite his habit and his deranged way of dressing, looks different.*

In fact, despite the mess of the old man, he has a very refined, relaxed, and natural posture. His legs are crossed in the style of an aristocrat of British royalty. On his thighs, he has arranged a newspaper, the pages of which he smiles at—a bit sarcastically it seems.

"I swear he's making fun of the newspaper news," Paquito mumbles. Moreover, he feels the curiosity to understand more clearly the situation of the individual, but at the same time, he doubts he should give such importance to the matter. He shakes his head. "That's not me."

Paquito concludes his rumination and then removes his gaze from the old man. Despite his young age, his aspirations in life go far beyond living under those conditions of mediocrity, hogwash, and limitations like that in which the old man lives.

Once again, the boy arrives at his job site. Enthusiastically, he begins his work and meets the obligations of the day. Step by step, he works to achieve in the near future what he has always dreamed of: success, reaching the top of the mountain, having a big house—maybe a mansion—a limousine, and a driver to take him and serve him. He's already imagined this; he imagines it all the time. A driver with gloves made of white silk and a kepi on his head, smartly dressed, reaches to open the door as if Paquito were a prime minister or something like that.

Paquito makes his way back to his apartment, returning to do what he does every late afternoon in his young life: paint. Like any boy his age, he has in his bedroom some posters of his artists of preference and paintings hanging on the wall; some of the paintings are copies of famous painters' works but also some originals of his own. Attending his artistic delirium with a few brushstrokes, the boy ends the day with one of the paintings that he has been working on. Then he drops on the bed, sleeping as a little lamb.

The next morning arrives, and Paquito wakes up somewhat nervous and agitated; it seems he has woken from a nightmare. He gets out of bed and fulfills his morning tasks. He goes on and takes a seat in the dining room. Mrs. Rosa, as usual, serves his breakfast.

"Good morning, Paquito. Are you all right? I notice you are quiet," Mrs. Rosa says.

"Yes, Mom," Paquito replies after being interrupted from his deep concentration. "I had a dream about Dad."

"Again?"

"Yes, and it's always the same; or rather, it is always something that has to do with what will happen in the future. In these dreams, I only see his face, but there is always regret, crying, sorrow, as if he were alive and suffering from having abandoned us."

"Paquito! We don't have to talk about those kinds of things now that he left us. Your dad was a good man, with delicate feelings, and you know, we don't really know what happened to him. Now, take your breakfast. It's getting late," his mother insists.

Paquito nods and eats.

Already more appeased and with better countenance, Paquito leaves the apartment. As always, he is ready to work, willing to fight the new day and live the same scenarios as usual: the neighbors, the noise, the trucks, the businesses opening their doors for work, and so on. That morning, adorned with beautiful foliage, beautiful gardens that border the surroundings, and a soft, fine air that inspires freedom, does not impress the boy. His goal of becoming rich and famous in the future monopolizes all his attention.

Once Paquito arrives at the train station, he boards the train and carries a newspaper under his arm. He opens it—to the business section, to be exact—and surveys the economic data and the development of the stock exchange in those early morning hours.

It's not more than a few minutes before, once again, the train makes a stop at the wrong time— an interruption very similar to the one it made a few days before. The unexpected stop does not draw the attention of most of the passengers on the train, but it does draw that of Paquito, who pauses his reading, raises his head, and directs his gaze through one of the gratings. When encountering the stare of the scruffy gentleman he saw just days before, every hair on his skin bristles. And despite the distance between him and the stranger, Paquito senses that those tired eyes distinguish him from the crowd, that they are fixed on him. He loosens his fingers and nearly drops the newspaper because of the strong shock. Paquito abruptly diverts his eyes from that of the old man, seeking to avoid another encounter and shelter his emotions. It is so creepy and confusing, the shared gaze between Paquito and the old man. Paquito silently struggles for some way to downplay what happened. He regains his balance, calms down, and tries to continue reading where he left off; ignoring the situation may be the best option. But the boy cannot shake from his mind the image that remains of that strange, cold, direct look the stranger gave him.

"It has to be pure coincidence," the boy murmurs.

"What else could it be? I can't be so naive to believe in predestinations, being the one chosen by the highest and that kind of nonsense many people believe."

Unless...

And abruptly, the train interrupts him and begins to speed up. At the same rate—although with reluctance and discretion—Paquito seeks the individual but sees no one; the elderly man is gone.

"He disappeared quickly," Paquito says, referring to the old man, then retakes his seat.

The rest of the day is like any other of his many weekdays on the job site, spent collaborating with many of his colleagues he does not like and others that he does—it simply makes no difference in his life. Later, at home, when the sun leaves that stage of light and warmth that enriches the day, he lies down and falls asleep.

The voice of a speaker of a morning news broadcast carries throughout the apartment. Thus begins a new day in the life of the restless and optimistic Paquito, who jumps out of bed, goes to the bathroom, and washes up. He has not even finished putting his pants on when his cell phone rings. He takes the call. It is his friend Aldo. Although there are European aspects in his facial structure, Aldo has tangled hair, is tall, and his complexion is light brown like most Latinos of the Caribbean. Aldo is of an age not so different from Paquito, who is perhaps a few months older than the enthusiastic Aldo. He has been a friend to Paquito since childhood—the kind of friend who, because of destiny, ends up being more a confidant and brother than a simple neighbor or friend.

"Hey, Aldo What's up?" Paquito asks.

Aldo says something on the other end of the line.

"All right, then," Paquito says. "I am going to pass by your house. We have to get together and talk about business and stuff. It's not a good move to continue this bullshit of being employed and enduring the demands of a frustrated boss who can't do any better." He laughs and adds, "So, I'll see you there."

Then, Paquito hangs up the phone and walks to Aldo's house, which is located just a couple of blocks from his place.

"Tell me, brother, what is it?" Aldo says when Paquito arrives at his home and opens the door a few minutes later.

Paquito enters the house, shakes Aldo's hands, and says hello to Mrs. Gloria and Mr. Rudy Goya, Aldo's parents, who seem to be dealing with their budget or house bills and expenses. Paquito also makes a signal of salute to the two younger kids sitting in the living room watching TV; they are Aldo's brother and sister.

"Well, as I told you," Paquito says while walking toward Aldo's bedroom, "I'm tired of working for others."

"Okay, I got that, so who are we going to kill, Paquito?"

Aldo's characteristic joking does not surprise Paquito, who knows his friend is joshing most of the time, even now when Aldo vaguely translates into English a popular Spanish phrase that means "What do we have to sacrifice in order to achieve the goal?"

"I think we are wasting time, Aldo. Time passes!" Paquito lets his hands fall to his sides. "We have too much talent that we cannot neglect. If we continue like this, we'll end up like those employees we're around all the time—slaves and penniless. With some luck, we'll survive long enough to get one of those retirement funds the company and the government give you after you've been fucked for a lifetime—after working like crazy for thirty, sometimes even more than forty years.

Aldo smiles; he has always seen Paquito as a natural leader.

"Why work for another guy if we can do our own business? Just imagine, Aldo: money, luxury cars, parties, and expensive, sophisticated drinks like champagne, French wines, and whiskeys, plus the best of foods like prawns! If this were our way of life, we could work even harder and for a longer time if necessary."

"Okay, Paquito, but…how do we start?"

"Don't worry, Aldo. That's not difficult at all. Let's start by looking to see where the money is, since money is what we want, and then we'll see how to get it. But for that, we have to use our heads. Don't you forget what they say: *Who huddles near a good tree, a good shade shelters him*," Paquito says, referring to a famous Spanish proverb that refers to the benefits and opportunities you get from socializing with powerful people.

"But, Paquito, money is everywhere. What we should be thinking about is what are we going to sell, because I'm guessing that's what you're planning on, right? To sell something? We also have to meet and interact with people of influence, like you say, people of money and power." Without waiting to see his friend's reaction, Aldo adds, "But for that we must introduce ourselves; what I mean is, we have to find a way to appear to be important people. You know that, Paquito—to reach people like that, you cannot present yourself as a simple employee or an assistant at a mediocre company."

"I think you're onto something, my friend!"

Paquito jokes now, and Aldo laughs along with him.

"And after we get all these things—cars, luxury homes, things like that—imagine how many hot girls we're going to be able to hang out with." Aldo is so excited that he exposes his real intentions.

"All in due time, Aldo. We are going to make an agenda; let's set a day, and together, we will study the market. We will see what the greatest demand is these days—first, in the neighborhood or the city, at the local level. It's very important to see what kind of marketing strategy will be best to put into action."

"That's right. Let's put it on the agenda right now, Paquito." Both take a deep breath and smile, and enthusiastically Aldo suggests, "But in the meantime, we are having a drink of whiskey. We are celebrating! How do you want it? With ice? Or, sorry, I mean"—he laughs—"on the rocks? Let's talk like high-class people now. With soda? You tell me."

It seems like the boys are reaching a more concrete idea of what their future should be like and how they should start up with a plan. They motivate each other and also celebrate.

"Go, brother…toast to our success!" Aldo says, raising a four-ounce glass with whiskey on the rocks, and Paquito does the same. With their arms up, they bump the drinks, causing that typical sound between glasses of iced-cold drinks, both smiling with confidence. A couple of hours are spent with the boys sharing ideas between sips and citing and consulting some books on personal motivation they have read. Before Paquito departs, they decide to meet again soon to continue with their plans.

The afternoon dazzles, and the horizon becomes shrouded in shadow. The night puts an end to a day that is already fatigued. And under that absolute darkness, the young Paquito, in a total exhaustion, arrives at his apartment, has his dinner, and then goes to his bedroom, where he droops to his bed, settles his head on the pillow, and sleeps.

The next morning arrives, and Paquito sits at the kitchen table ready for breakfast. As usual, he says good morning to his mom and chats with her. The story that he brings up now has nothing to do with the dreams of the previous night but is about that gentleman he saw a couple of times from the metro. His mother listens to him but is not giving too much of her attention. She responds naturally and even asks related questions to make sure Paquito does not feel disregarded, when really, she is more concerned that they both leave the house without delay. But she smiles while serving two fried eggs, bread, and milk to him. Once they finish with breakfast, they stand up. Paquito gives a kiss to his mom and says goodbye. Mrs. Rosa does the same, leaving the apartment after Paquito.

That day, like any other day of the week, will pass without major surprises, but the weekend will prove to be life-altering.

On Saturday, in the evening hours, Paquito feels very bored at home. He's in no mood to paint or to read anything. His mind wanders, looking for ideas, but nothing comes to him, and so he gets up from his favorite chair and leaves the apartment. He goes for a walk. Walking is not exactly his favorite hobby, but it is better than nothing on that autumn day. It's a wet and cold afternoon, but, as if decorated with the magic and precision of the brushstroke of an impressionist painter, the greenery and bushes add charm to the romantic and temperate setting. Paquito is pensive, as usual, and careless, easily surrendering his mind to anything that could distract a boy of his age.

Paquito walks a few minutes and arrives at a small but beautiful gazebo adorned with red tiles worn out by time. The gazebo is centered among beautiful herbage and elegant iron benches that circulate the small park. There is no one there since the afternoon is damp and cold. Vaguely, he looks around and moves to the bottom of the square. He notices that, at the end, there toward the other side of the park, is a mountain with tall flowered trees, and that within that forest, hidden and at a distance, is the site where he saw the elderly man—the man who looked straight into his eyes. The same man that—though Paquito doesn't like to admit it—has mysteriously stolen much of his attention. Paquito hesitates for a moment; he isn't sure whether he wants to get closer to that hovel or just forget about the whole thing and go back home.

"But this whole thing is so weird!" he whispers to himself while he angles his head curiously to look at part of the wall and door of the old man's house. He remains there for a few seconds, changes his positioning a couple of times, looks back at the house, then twists his face and finally squares and prepares to turn; he has decided to go back.

But then he feels dripping water on his shoulders. Paquito looks up, trying to see where the drops are coming from, and it is then that a tremendous downpour begins to fall. Paquito turns his gaze toward the park, looking for shelter and thinks of the gazebo, but it is not close enough. His common sense tells him that the best shelter from the rain would be under the trees on the other side of the square, inside the mountain where the stranger's house is. Paquito races to the spot, where he falls under a walnut tree. The tree is large and bushy, and its trunk is wide and strong, big enough to shelter him from the copious rain that falls over the area.

He is now closer to the house of the old man, and occasionally, he looks up, his curiosity increasingly evident. But Paquito also feels distrust and prefers to keep his distance from those who seem incompatible and or irrelevant to his lifestyle.

"Generally, people living in these conditions are troubled or crazy people, people with turbulent pasts. Losers," he mutters and convinces himself that he has made the right decision not to approach.

The old man stops crying. He is interrupted by the rain that falls on the reckless life of all. He moves closer to the window, ready to be happy. He wears a smile, watching the waterfall copiously, and even extends his arms to touch it and feel it on his hands; he seems to be lost in that feeling of happiness. He looks to the outside, and his eyes serve him a landscape full and serene, but most importantly, company.

"It seems as if the rain scares you."

The voice behind Paquito startles him a little. He turns around, and there he is—the same old man of two mornings, the man he's seen from the subway but has not been able to see closely until now. He notes his advanced age, about seventy-five years. Paquito looks at him directly and notices they are of a very similar stature. The man has medium-long gray hair and a short gray beard.

"Hello, sir."

"Come in, boy, so you don't get wet." Without letting go of that smile, strong and sure, the old man offers him in.

"Thank you, sir." The invitation takes Paquito by surprise, but the boy accepts since the rain remains copious and invariable.

Paquito hurries and enters the small house, crossing the house's small gallery and stepping across yellowish, dry, and wet leaves. There are a couple of old rocking chairs made of South American white pine at one side of the arched gallery. It is a small house but well built. Its walls are a combination of natural brick and limestone. Its main door is pure mahogany and finely chiseled. The floor is classic mosaics of black and white, a Gothic style but corroded by neglect and time. It is evident from all the dust how old and neglected the house is; that much can be seen from afar.

"Sit down and relax. I want you to have tea with me—the kind of tea I often make from these leaves and roots. Sorry for the way I am. I didn't even ask; I know." He smiles so wide that it almost covers his entire face. "I've been your age and mine. I have the experience this time has allowed me to have; that is, I am almost certain that drinking hot and healthy is the best."

"Yes, I think tea would be fine. Thank you."

The old man listens as Paquito tells him his favorite drink is not exactly tea, but coffee. But the boy accepts and sits in a chair made of wood and leather, very similar to the one he has in his room but much older.

The strange man walks toward the rear of the house and disappears; it seems he has gone to the patio. Paquito takes advantage and snoops around the room. There are some tables against the wall and old lamps made of copper. The living room has two large windows, elongated and covered by thick curtains that fall to the floor. The curtains are dark purple and Louis XVI style that greatly limit sunlight. Paquito is very interested in some of the drawings and several oil paintings the old man has hung on the walls. There are even some painting materials and brushes inside a big container made of clay on an iron table at the back of the room. He likes what he sees and even feels at home with some of the work the old man has there.

"I would even dare to say that we have a similar style," murmurs Paquito.

"Have you settled yet? Hey, I haven't even asked your name, boy," the old man says when he unexpectedly returns to the room, a little wet and shaking off the water.

"My name is Paquito, sir, and my last name is Dauhajre."

The man puts on a soft smile. "You can call me Mr. Frank, Paquito, and get ready...you're going to have the best tea you've ever drank in your life." Mr. Frank stands tall with pride and a smile of arrogance. "It is made by the hands of God himself, son, in one of his many inspirations.

Call it nature if it suits you more. These are eucalyptus leaves and soursop leaves that I collected from the patio—pure organic, as they call it today, though it is what was once normal."

After sparing a few more words, the stranger goes back to the kitchen and gets the tea; it is served in a beautiful white porcelain cup, and he serves it with all of the proper protocols and procedures.

Definitely a sloppy guy with class, Paquito thinks. "Thank you," he says. "I was looking at the paintings while you were back there. They're very beautiful. Do you know that I also like to paint?"

"Thank you, boy. I have tried my best. Not all of them are so pretty, but neither are they too bad, you know? There is always an occasional imperfection or error in them, like in many things we do." Looking pensive, the old man examines one of the paintings. "But, I would say that more important than their beauty is the meaning they provide and communicate. The interesting thing about art and paintings, in particular, is precisely the way they express themselves; they can do this in the coloring, with their lines, with brushstrokes, with their landscapes. In the end, it is the secret of the art itself."

Both undertake and develop an extensive and enjoyable conversation. Having had an understanding from the beginning, they find it simple enough to open up to each other. They talk about trivial things, and the initial mistrust is felt less in the boy, who relaxes and gets comfortable in the armchair. Paquito tells Mr. Frank about his family—Mrs. Rosa and her affairs. The old man is interested. He listens carefully, but despite the courtesy and dedication he is lent, Paquito remains, to an extent, reserved. He details some of the artworks to Mr. Frank and tries to interpret the meaning of some of them.

He points to one on the wall. "I think I recognize that painting you have over there."

"He is a famous impressionist painter, son." The old man refers to the painting's artist.

"Of course, he is very famous. I know him very well. He is Pierre Bonnard," Paquito says proudly. Mr. Frank responds with a small smile. "At the beginning, of course, because I was a young guy, I just gave importance to the colors—if I liked them—and tried to limit my criticism of the neatness of the lines. I know you understand what I'm saying. I couldn't find the message or reach the imagination of the artist or, in this case, Bonnard's mind. When I understood his depth and what he wanted to communicate on the canvas, I was so impressed and amazed that I even began to relate him with mankind and then to understand life much better—the reality of the real."

"I guess you mean that he painted by imagination," Paquito adds to the old man's comments, to which he responds with his classic half smile.

Paquito notes that, in the distance, there is an adjoining wall, and there is something hanging on the wall that also seems to be a painting, but it is covered by a white cloth of fine linen. Paquito restrains from asking; he doesn't have enough confidence to ask about something the old man obviously wants to hide.

Then he observes another one that awakens his attention as well. It is not finished, but he can tell that it seeks to give an interesting and strange message. "This one is weird," Paquito says, regarding the other piece. "Sorry for saying it like that, but it is simple and deep at the same time,"

"Why the curiosity, son? It is a simple job, and it is not even finished yet, as you can see. But it seems as if someone cracked da Vinci's style, right?" the old man jokes, hinting at the symbols da Vinci used in his artworks. "But in this painting, I have just painted a tree with large roots and a little bird on one of the branches."

"Something tells me that it has a special meaning to you. Am I wrong?" Paquito insists.

"No, son. Let me explain it to you."

After a short pause, the old man continues. "This piece—I call it *Freedom*. It may sound paradoxical somehow. A tree that is always planted there, anchored in one place, and yet I call it *Freedom*, right? Well, for me, freedom can be a relative matter. It may even be the conclusion many thinkers and philosophers have reached—that true freedom is inside you. I think this is important for those of us who are part of human society to acknowledge. Freedom is determined by what you think, how you think, who you follow, and how you do things. Regardless of the benefits we have in life—travel, vacation, shopping, money.—if you do not open your mind, you will remain a prisoner to the material things and the beliefs you have inherited from your family and the culture too. They are the ones that dictate your consciousness or your subconscious, and many of them do nothing but follow a very strong pattern of prejudices."

Extending a smile, he continues, saying, "Many of the people who give you a hand when you are defeated or give you a piece of bread because you look scruffy and dirty don't always do it because they are good people. Instead, they do it to feel good about themselves. We humans feel a great spiritual relief when doing so, and our pride fills us up. That is, we do a favor more for our own well-being than for the welfare of others."

"Oh, interesting," Paquito says, bored and uncaring that the old man has no coordination in what he says. "But I would be somewhat difficult to control, Mr. Frank. We all depend on what you call prejudice or pattern, which is what we learn in our homes and in the schools. But how can anyone distinguish when it is cultural prejudice, as you say, and when it is not?"

The old man smiles slightly and looks at him. "You are not very religious, right?" asks Paquito.

The old man laughs. "Well…that depends on what you mean by being 'religious,' young man. It seems to me that every creed has the same purpose, and that is to believe in a supreme being—in God. And the truth is that believing in one god, regardless of which one, and in another life after this one on earth, will undoubtedly give you more peace of mind and hope while you're here." He gazes at nothing and shifts to an attitude of disapproval. "It's more than enough to appease the cowardice mankind suffers from. As for me, I can tell you that I can believe in creation the same way I believe in destruction."

He looks down to the spot where Paquito is sitting and sees that the boy now looks confused, perhaps because he speaks of destruction or maybe because of the way in which he has expressed it— so different from the way the great majority of the people in Paquito's few years of life have addressed it.

"But how is it that what any ordinary person normally sees as a creation of God, someone else can see as the result of destruction?" Paquito wonders aloud.

"I believe that superior life form or super powerful energy, in one way or another, has to do with all that we see in the universe and all that we have on earth, an omnipotent being to which each group has given a different name and has seated in unequal places. I imagine we do this according to convenience and our power of discernment. These different disciplines—if that's what you would call them to distinguish them—have developed systems adapted to the groups' respective needs. But of all these things, in my opinion, the intellectual part is the one that can best help to open your eyes, to understand. This is a process that requires you to take your mind to a certain level of development—an appropriate mental level, I mean—where you can ultimately get rid of taboos and beliefs inherited from your ancestors, especially those who come from the countryside, people who never had the opportunity to study and so time has kept them cornered."

Mr. Frank turns and walks through the room. "That is when you begin to understand and see things from your own judgment and from an analytical capacity." He puffs up and cracks an ill-timed smile. "There are even theories out there that go much further; they encourage you to be afraid, even to doubt. And I can assure you, my young friend, that there is no tool more effective than that—fear, it kills your curiosity."

He pauses, and again, he appears lost in his mind, but then he picks the subject back up. "It is where the phrase *curiosity killed the cat* comes from." He looks at Paquito and laughs. "This is what many people from the countryside in Latin America say when someone is so nosey that they get into problems or even get killed."

He smiles a more open smile and says, "That, my dear friend, is my favorite. Fear has even been a subject of discussion among philosophers, politicians, and strategists of the world to manipulate the masses." He looks inspired. "Niccolò Machiavelli, for example."

He meets Paquito's gaze. "I imagine you've heard of him? He is one of the most famous and recognized philosophers and politicians in this world. Fear, unfortunately, is effective. I think to myself, and sometimes, I am overwhelmed. Why not teach people through education, right?

Or through affection and love? It sounds romantic. Just like Martin Luther King Jr. wrote once in his book *Strength to Love*, it would be a beautiful thing. Instead, people who have experienced faithfulness or loyalty are more easily manipulated by fear than by any other means."

He concludes his monologue, then stands so still he seems to have become a shop dummy.

"I agree with you," Paquito says. "Fear is one of the great enemies of the successful man. But the thing about rain is just the discomfort of getting wet. You then have to change clothes, and you can even catch a cold because of it."

"Looks like the rain has already waned," the old man says, interfering with Paquito's train of thought. He has a disoriented, cold look about him.

"Yes? And how can you tell, if you have not even looked out?"

Mr. Frank returns to himself and says, "By the smell, kid. The air you feel when it's raining is not the same air as when it has finished raining. It is as if the earth has been united with the air—kind of like steam. Or maybe it's the heat under the ground that then evaporates when it gets wet and rises."

He furrows a brow. "But I don't know…is it the same? I'm not a scientist, but I imagine that something like that is what causes the feeling and smell. I think it's one of the things you learn thanks to old age and not in school."

The old man smiles, as if enjoying the moment of analysis. He crosses his legs and has another sip of hot tea. He also turns on a small music device that he has near his seat and places a CD inside; it is a cheerful instrumental piece called "Pearl Fishers" by Paul Mauriat. A quiet Paquito watches him. The old man is gone, deep in thought but happy.

The boy looks around the house, and his eyes return to that painting covered by the white linen. He again feels a lot of desire to ask about it but remains silent; again, he feels that it would be inappropriate to question the matter. *It's so obvious that whatever is under that thing is a secret of his.*

"Well, Don..." Paquito improvises, getting up from the seat. It dawns on him that he doesn't really know this man who, with such kindness and courtesy, received him in his house.

The old man smiles and stands up to say goodbye. "Don't complicate yourself, son. Just call me Mr. Frank, like I told you."

They shake hands, and Paquito walks toward the exit while the old man serves as an escort. He opens the door, and as the old man said, it is no longer raining.

"Thank you for your attention and for the tea,

Mr. Frank."

The old man stands against the doorframe watching Paquito go with a rare smile from ear to ear. The complacency on his face is obvious—and all for having been able to share this short time with someone so special, even if it was a stranger.

Sitting on a wooden chair in a local cafeteria not too far from where she lives—and at the same time Paquito is finishing his encounter with Mr. Frank—Mrs. Rosa shares a cup of coffee with her co-worker Amparo, also an immigrant from Argentina. It is a break time at work, and the ladies discuss trivial things, such as the end of a television soap opera they both watch every night in their respective homes.

"And to think that Rodolfo looks so much like Virgilio," Rosa says with a sigh, referring to and comparing her missing husband to the handsome protagonist in the TV soap opera they follow.

"Really, do you think?" Amparo purses her lips. "Well, Rosa, better if we don't start talking about things that don't matter anymore. At the end of the day, that just makes life bitter, and that's not a good idea, friend."

"I know, but it's hard to help. It hurts when you lose someone. I have lost other relatives apart from Virgil. When someone you love dies, at least you usually know where the person is buried and how they died. But with Virgil—who was a normal and very good man, you know—that was not the case. He just vanished.

"I understand, Rosa. When I was very young, I had a cousin who disappeared without a trace. My Aunt Rita, her mother, she was never the same. She never recovered from the loss, and then she got sick because of it. Poor aunt of mine, she died just a few years ago; she was already a very old and skinny woman." Amparo shakes off the bad memories. "Are you sure there was nothing unusual about Virgil? Maybe he was a good man, but...you know, many have their weaknesses too. I wouldn't want to put bad things on your mind either..." Amparo tilts her head.

"Still, maybe he had an enemy—a politician or something like that. He wasn't sick, right?"

"No, Amparo."

"Whatever it is, my friend, we must also take into account that time has passed; that was already many years ago, Rosa. Now you have to think about you. Do you understand? We are not twenty years old, nor are we as attractive as before. There is little time left, and we have to rebuild our lives now while we can. Your child is already grown.

And even if he feels weird, jealous, or whatever in the beginning, in the long run, he will understand and adapt to a new partner of yours. Cheer up, woman. Don't be silly!"

"You know, Amparito, Paquito is only twenty years old. He is not too young anymore, I know that, but still, he didn't even see me with his dad. He was barely three years old when Virgil disappeared, and I don't think he remembers from that age. I don't believe it's time yet, and I hope that he is at least a few years older before he starts asking questions." Rosa exhibits a change of attitude, with a lighthearted look and a smile, she adds, "So, as for when that new good-looking man will come around—I can wait a little bit longer."

Amparo smiles back. "Good, friend," she says, looks at her watch, and realizes the break time is up. "Time's up. We better hustle." And both stand up and go back to work.

Paquito arrives at his apartment a short time after having a long conversation with Mr. Frank and goes into his bedroom. He looks closely at some of the paintings he's made and compares them with those he saw in the old man's house— the colors, types of landscapes, and brushstrokes of each one of them, everything he's painted with gestures of happiness. He feels something special about meeting and sharing with the old man, who he may already view as a new and good friend.

He enjoys thinking over his conversations with Mr. Frank. Paquito learned something from him, and he thinks he could enjoy his time with the old man in a different way than he does with those already in his daily life. But he feels exhausted now and lies on the bed and places his head on the pillow. His eyes blink, and he closes them, then opens them; it is not exactly the time to go to sleep yet. Out over the horizon, rays of the sun still filter through. He feels a little cold and slips between the sheets. His eyelids fall slowly, and he is lost in absolute comfort...

The streets are unpaved and covered with dust. The tender boy, all skin and bones, races along them. He has no awareness of hurting himself or being barefoot, much less of getting sunburned with the little clothes he wears. He is a perfect creature that does not understand responsibility or aspirations, which for him, are still unknown. That naive fear of losing the sprint competition against other children in the neighborhood weighs on him, but he also enjoys those extraordinary feelings that only infancy and innocence can allow.

That anxiety becomes pure joy upon reaching the final goal; the boy skeleton of just six years old ends up getting first place in the race. He jumps and shares hugs between his friends and neighbors who witnessed everything. He celebrates and laughs like crazy.

"I win! I am the champion!" The boy shouts and shouts, and because of the ecstasy overflowing him, he is detached from the group.

On the run home, he doesn't think straight until he reaches his apartment, and even then, he is unworried about the reprimand he will receive from his mother when she sees the state he's in. He enters and crosses like a comet through the living room, looking sideways at his mother, whose eyes widen when she sees he's a whole mess, sweaty and with ruffled hair. His heart stops, and all the excitement he brought home is transformed into uncertainty. But then comes a bucket of cold water that falls on him, and now the child enjoys a bath in a beautiful river of warm and crystalline waters. His body is fresh, and the boy savors the swim in those tropical waters.

"Paquito. Paquito!"

He awakens with a fright. Mrs. Rosa is sitting on one side of the bed and has woken him from that exciting and pleasant dream this late afternoon.

"Hi, Mom. How was work?" he asks with a heavy tongue because he is still half-drunk with sleep.

"Fine, son, but I'm dead tired! These Saturdays are tough, but at least it's the last day of the week." Slowly, Paquito stands up and stretches, opening his arms to wake up completely. "And you just arrived? What time is it? Whoa! I had very nice dreams, Mom. It was like I had returned to the past. Like when I was a very new boy."

"Oh, yes? You really dream, my boy. So, tell me, what happened in this one now?"

"Nothing special. It was more how I felt in the dream. Freaking out like any other young boy in the neighborhood I was born in. I enjoyed everything very much. There was a strong sun itch, and I even enjoyed that. Running like crazy, even without shoes on, I was like a locomotive without brakes. I ran barefoot up the streets of the neighborhood, which were old and full of holes, but I didn't care."

He smiles as he recounts his dream. "During the dream, I felt so energetic, like I could even fly above everyone. And then—you know how dreams are—I saw myself in a different place. I was swimming. It was a river that, if I'm not mistaken, looked a lot like one we and the whole family went to once. I think you took us, Mom. At that age, I didn't know how to swim; however, in the dream, I swam like a fish."

"Well, if a dream is a good one and doesn't hurt you, go with it!" Mrs. Rosa says as she gets off the bed and walks out of the room. As a mother, she has barely arrived at the apartment after an arduous day of work, and while weary, she goes to the kitchen to see what she is going to cook for dinner. Paquito also gets up from bed and follows after picking up a book. It is the same personal motivational book that he always reads. As a boy, he is not worried about his mother's sacrifices. He is not fully aware of how hard it is for a single mother to go out to work six days a week, for ten hours a day, then come home to cook, scrub the dishes that are dirty, clean the apartment, and find the time to talk to Paquito and give him the support young men his age sometimes need.

Those last rays of sun lost their glare, and the dark waves of that tired sky become increasingly axiomatic. Night falls, and Paquito keeps reading and learning about how to succeed in life. His imagination turns, and he sees himself enjoying the life of luxuries and splendor that success will bring him: extravagant mansions, long limousines, exotic parties, impressive swimming pools, and an office with all the magnificence possible. It's the same picture he always carries in his head—his real dream.

If his dream does not come to fruition, it would puncture him greatly; but perhaps, it would help him to reflect and make him a better person in the long run. For now, his mind is overloaded with ambition. Paquito follows the advice of a co-worker who has told him about a new way to do business on his own, and he sees it as a very good opportunity that he should not let go, and without much thought, he grabs that opportunity. He renounces his job, and with the money from the settlement, which by law, he is entitled to from the company, makes an investment. He is convinced by all of the books and marketing motivators he's read and followed along the years that have persuaded him it will go all right.

From that chimera image, the figure of his new friend, Mr. Frank, arrives. This simple memory turns Paquito's emotions upside down, and he feels confused. He notes the many things that differentiate him from the elderly man; he is much more ambitious than him. He also feels uneasy, because even though he liked the conversation and the company of the old man, he fears the possibly negative influence Mr. Frank could have in his life and his goals. And so he tries to forget Mr. Frank, but his image comes back in his mind again. Paquito puts the book aside and goes to the kitchen for dinner, hoping a good meal will calm the strange mental intervention he suffers.

The light is very poor, religiously following the pattern dictated by the time. Faithfully, Mr. Frank takes care of himself and serves a hot cup of tea in his sophisticated French cup. He relaxes and does not show much of his feelings. He exists within himself, and his gaze is fixed and cold, as it normally is. He crosses his legs and adjusts himself, then takes a sip. He gets to his feet. In that old stereo, he plays his favorite musical piece again:

"Pearl Fishers." He moves to the window.

It is already very dark outside. On the windowsill, Mr. Frank rests the two elbows of his arms. He closes his eyes when he feels the caress of a long breeze that enters through the port, then opens them, then closes them. It seems he is looking for something. Perhaps he is homesick. Perhaps he is lonely, noiseless with no one to talk to.

A couple of days have passed since Paquito and Aldo met up, and Paquito gives him a call. They set a meeting to talk about the business.

"Hey, Paquito. What's up?" Full of enthusiasm, Aldo salutes Paquito.

"I am doing fine, brother. How about you? Ready to get whatever you want in life?" Paquito smiles. "I was reading some biographies of successful people and also about the way some companies have been doing their businesses lately. Let me tell you, my friend, we're probably not going to need as much money to start our own company as we thought in the beginning."

"And how is that, Paquito?"

Paquito tells him about this company that is very rich and growing. Aldo listens and seems to be satisfied with his friend's idea.

"So, it won't be our company exactly, but we'll be like an associate of it?"

"Don't forget...we don't have to compete, especially when we don't have enough capital to start with against the strong and rich. But we can be a part of them. Collaborating with them to start will be easier. It's like an old Chinese philosopher once said: *Never loses who never competes.*

Aldo laughs while Paquito looks at him with total satisfaction.

And this is how the young friends start working in business. The plan is to under-contract other executive vendors or associates of business, which is the best way to cater to a salesperson's ego, and divide the points or earnings among all parties.

A couple of months go by. Paquito and Aldo are already experiencing growth, but some issues come up. It seems growing is not the most difficult part of a business; maintaining that growth is a different matter. While some associates of their group did not last long, others are still coming to the group, but these newcomers are always small in numbers. Still, Paquito and Aldo try harder, always motivating each other, until the day they feel too exhausted and the enthusiasm they had in the beginning is long gone.

"Well, what do we do now, Paquito?" Aldo regards Paquito in a café near their neighborhood.

"Don't worry, Aldo. Things happen, and this doesn't have to be the last page of our story. Let's see what might come up later. Relax, bro!"

Paquito invites him to drink from the glass of beer on the table. So, there are the boys— depressed, sharing some beers and talking about things not much related to business. They are trying to forget the whole bad experience they've had and do so until the day comes to an end and both of the good friends head home.

Once at home, Paquito takes a shower and gets in bed, expecting to sleep well and have a different and better tomorrow.

The boys are still standing despite their failure. The fears and regret experienced have made a difference on the guys' lives, but this state of pain has somehow also united them. Nothing links two people so much as living through a bad experience. A single week is enough for Paquito to reconsider his faith and to decide, one more time, to pave the way for a new investment, but not without letting his inseparable friend, Aldo, again be part of it. It is a new opportunity to achieve a dream that already seems part of their nature, their blood, their DNA, their souls. When they agree to give it another go, it is almost an oath, a contract signed with blood. Yes, the enthusiasm is back.

"Aldo, we have to prepare a promotion, so we have to contact the press. Yes…a press conference, something well done that looks like something great. A thing that will impress."

"You are very right, Paquito, but we have to put our failures behind us. Let's give this a lot of optimism." Aldo replies with the enthusiasm these popular motivational books usually leave in the youth and in any vulnerable mind.

They make new plans and prepare for their execution; this includes marketing strategy and anything that will secure profits or money.

It's not long before they began to see good results. They are already seeing a lot of money coming in, and they rush to reinvest it. As advised by their leaders and many of those books and manuals on strategies, they put some of the income into their personal image and the presentation of the company. They go shopping and buy brand-new clothes. They also finance a couple of beautiful brand-new vehicles. Always executive style. All the while, they socialize and make contacts with other entrepreneurs, which, according to their beliefs, should help expand their businesses and become more competitive.

Thus, they keep going in this way, and a flow of money keeps coming in. But it is not enough to spend the money on clothing and cars, so the boys also use it for vacationing.

Regardless of all the experience they think they have, they allow the spaces between work and free time to become unbalanced and have to resort to bank loans and even relatives and partners for money. Such a situation causes a greater economic commitment, but if they have any savings in their account, it is not enough. Their crisis harmonizes with a decline in the stock market, and therefore, the sales are reduced and then freeze.

"Paquito, what do we do now?"

"I think this is a test. It's best to wait."

"But we have people who are getting desperate to be paid."

Paquito, being the leader of the group of businessmen, pauses. He says nothing, just thinks, calculating, trying to find a solution to the problem. He then looks back at his desperate friend and says, "We still have some money, but we can't use the little we have to pay our debts. Remember, Aldo, if we pay, we are left with two things: bankruptcy and the inability to get someone to lend to us again."

Aldo nods, Paquito's words giving him strength. "Now is not the time to decide anything." Assured, Paquito makes good use of his well-learned capitalist philosophy. "We relax, and we do everything we do every day, as if nothing is going on. Tell everyone who asks you for payment that everything is fine, to be patient."

With a small smile, Paquito stands up and leaves.

When days pass with no recovery or improvement in the business, the two friends really start to worry. Investors and lenders take legal action. The fear that Paquito and Aldo now suffer is almost uncontrollable. They get depressed, and the depression persists even when they comfort each other and dry their tears. Now that their dream of achieving success has crumbled once again, their only hope is to get out of that dungeon healthy and alive. But it is not an easy thing. There are a few charges that weigh on them, and with no money to pay, thcy spend some time in jail—not to mention the desperation of the boy's parents confronting such a difficult task on their hands.

But some time passes by, and things turns around; one of those lenders sympathizes. Old friends and acquaintances of Paquito's mother and other relatives, also of Aldo, twisted his arm, did some errands, and spoke with those others affected, and arrived at agreements for extensions of payments through the courts. This makes it possible for the boys to finally get out of prison. The time they spent in that hell was not much, but for family boys, educated young adults, those days felt like years.

That attitude of determination and strength with which Paquito always bragged about his goals vanishes as soon as he arrives home. He walks straight into the shower and without taking his clothes off, gets into the bathtub and drops to the floor. He cries all his hidden tears while the water from the shower falls on his head. He squeezes his eyes and cries out the pain and weakness he had to keep hidden inside among the dirt, bad smells, thugs, and bandits.

Mrs. Rosa understands all this suffering, and despite being one of the many people Paquito never listened to when they tried to provide counsel, offers him the support and the necessary time required to work out his distress. She asks her son to relax and tells him that he doesn't have to worry about anything, because she will cover all the home expenses.

While life has not been so benevolent to Paquito, he does not resign from his dream to ensure a better future for him and his mother. But with everything he already tried to achieve some improvement in life, those efforts did not help, and only another job in the city with a better salary will do now that he's been back from prison for seventeen days. The whole situation has forced him to think more negatively with regard to business, and although he subconsciously still resists accepting such a reality, he progressively becomes discouraged.

Paquito wakes up and does what he does most of his days: complies at work, comes back home, takes a shower, puts on casual clothes, and has something to eat. When it's getting late in the afternoon, he feels sad and disoriented, but in spite of this, he picks a brush and sits, trying to find the inspiration to paint, but nothing comes to his mind...until the night arrives.

But this night is out of the ordinary. It's an overwhelming space of time, like those nights when you replay the entire story of your struggles and failures and allow them to roost between your temples, and you feel the desperate need for a few shots of whatever of drink you can reach to annihilate your existence, to disappear from such a miserable moment, to get drunk, to mourn, to open your soul to that strange and undesirable night and let it be your deaf companion. So, Paquito drops the brush he has in his hand and leaves the apartment, going somewhere to have a drink.

But Paquito is not the only one who arrives at the strange place called The Caporal. The Caporal is a bar in the neighborhood. Besides serving the typical food of the multi-ethnic area, it's also open for music and drinks of all kinds after midnight. Inside, Paquito takes a seat at the bar and asks for a whiskey on the rocks. As soon as the boy is served, he takes a long shot, shakes his head, and for a couple of seconds, closes his eyes in relief. In the space filled with few people lit by opaque light, Paquito sees a girl of cinnamon skin who is seated at the opposite corner of the bar. She looks thoughtful, but also he notices in her big eyes outlined in black a sad experience that is recent and persisting. The boy asks for a second drink and takes another long sip. He looks at the girl again and notices she is looking back.

They note each other from a distance, but the attraction Paquito may feel for the young woman mingles with bitterness and desolation, which is what's brought him to this place. He doesn't make direct eye contact with her to avoid showing any interest. No wonder bars are places mostly frequented by people who are suffering from depression or disappointment. The patrons are looking for shelter and comfort, for some kind of pleasure or company, but despite the grief that brought Paquito here, finding pleasure with a stranger is not the intention.

Three quarters of an hour elapse, and it is

the following shot on the rocks that subtly shakes Paquito's mood. Despite trying not to pay at-tention to the girl, he has gazed a few times and noticed that she has done the same thing—with proper discretion, of course. So, the boy gets up from his stool and walks toward the girl. He stands before her, and there they are now, looking each other directly in the eyes. They don't hurry to make introductions, and neither seems to be impressed. They are really two sleepwalkers who, with pure eyes, have understood each other perfectly.

"You don't know me, but we understand each other," Paquito says boldly and without hesitation, and this, unlike when he approached her, seems to impress the girl.

"Hi," she responds. "My name is Lucia. And you are?"

With all the calm in the world, Paquito tells her his name.

And so they start talking, a very simple and entertaining conversation, and gradually open up to each other. Between short stories and humorous tales, the bar fades and disappears around them because they are so concentrated on their conversation. They comfort one another by sharing family experiences and stories. But it seems to be Paquito who tells the funniest stories that make Lucia laugh so strongly. A couple of hours have already passed, and they begin feeling dizzy from so many drinks—mostly Paquito, who drank double or triple what Lucia did. It's much later, and both are exhausted but also relieved and happier than before they entered the bar. They decide to split, but not before exchanging telephone numbers, even though Lucia hesitates a little in the beginning. They also agree to see each other again and at a place to meet for a meal.

Paquito's apartment is not far from The Caporal. Despite his stumbling steps, he advances and smiles, remembering some of the moments he shared with Lucia that night. It is a very dark night, and nothing can be heard around, but there goes Paquito walking into it.Then, out of nowhere, he hears a gentle melody that pleases him. It seems every step he takes brings him closer to the music. It is strange and likewise marvels him, and soon it comes to him that it is the piece, cheerful and instrumental, he once listened to in the house of his friend Mr. Frank—"Pearl Fishers."

He dons a slight smile and hums the tuneful melody. But then Paquito startles, noting that he is not on the right path, but instead heading in the direction of the old man's house.

"Fuck!" he mutters. "I can't be this drunk…"

When Paquito looks behind him, he's struck with tremendous shock. There, barely two feet behind him, Mr. Frank stands, mostly expressionless but maybe somewhat disturbed.

"Mr. Frank!" Paquito yells.

The old man answers with a question: "Are you coming from where I think you are coming from?" Even more confused is Paquito; he did not expect to find his old friend roaming around at that hour of the early morning.

"There are situations that can lead us anywhere at random, but this does not mean such a moment is an opportunity. This is not your night, nor is that your friend," Mr. Frank adds.

"But, Mr. Frank, I did not expect you out here at this time. And how do you know about Lucia? Were you at the bar too?" With a scruffy voice, trying to keep his balance, Paquito asks this.

"You have three options in life: the world, loneliness, or yourself," Mr. Frank philosophizes. He doesn't add anything, only tilts his head. There's a humming in the thin air. Mr. Frank begins to whistle and walks in the opposite direction of Paquito, who walks his gaze toward the starry skies, though it is almost dawn.

Paquito is alone again and not even sure the old man had been there or if it was just his imagination. He feels even farther away from home, but he finally arrives at the apartment without problem. As soon as he gets there, he goes to his room and drops on the bed; there is not much more the tired boy needs than to collapse.

Paquito finds himself back in the exotic bar in his dreams. Below the romantic lights, his eyes stumble upon those big and beautiful ones of Lucia. This time, she's more willing. With delirium, he looks at her, and his heart sprouts with joy; it feels like a river overflowing from so much excitement. In fantastic and sudden ways, he meets with her robust breasts, which are so close to his body, and with their lips. They learn what living is. It is that maddening and abrupt feeling, the most sincere essence of the human being, and Paquito is not afraid. He clings to the feeling. It is unique, irreplaceable, and he will live and enjoy it in all its fullness. Their bodies meet, and they reveal each other. There are no more glasses of alcohol, only sweat, sheets, and the excitement of love and surrender. The background music blurs and merges with a duo of seductive screams that seem to have fallen from the sky.

Paquito wakes. His body is tired from such an unreal experience. He is lightened, happy, but more than that, he is filled with hope. He looks at the door of his room, making sure that no one is near or will suddenly enter. His sheets are smeared, and he strips them from the bed; likewise, he removes his underwear and throws them into the laundry basket.

He has slept for about ten hours, and the wooden clock hanging on the wall strikes 3:43 p.m. He goes straight to the bathtub for a refreshing shower and drinks as much water as possible out of dehydration. Paquito could eat a whole horse for breakfast, that's how hungry he is. Since his mother is not home—she has gone to work, just as she does every Saturday early in the morning—he fries a couple of eggs, cuts a good piece of Italian bread, and pours a glass of orange juice. It is the most practical and quick breakfast he can make.

While he eats, he thinks of Lucia. He looks for the piece of napkin she wrote her phone number on, finds it, and smiles. He considers calling her but then worries he'll seem desperate and decides to take a moment to do it later. He puts the little piece of napkin back into his pants pocket.

Mr. Frank's face comes to mind, and he remembers his words, specifically how he had warned him about the lush place of pleasures, about the drinks and Lucia. Paquito tries to erase that image from his mind, but he can't. It is as if the old man has seized his mind and dictates what he thinks and sees.

"That's weird! How can I be so influenced by

Mr. Frank?"

Making a decision all his own, he swipes up his phone and dials Lucia's cell phone number. The phone rings three times, and on the fourth ring, someone picks up; it's Lucia. Paquito feels relief and joy but doesn't allow that much emotion to enter his voice. They have a pleasant and long conversation and agree to meet soon.

The next day, Paquito leaves home in a rush to meet Lucia at a modest café in the area, not far from his neighborhood. They are nervous and greet each other with a peck, then Paquito asks Lucia to choose a table. She does so, and there they sit down. Once the waitress gets their orders and brings a cup of black coffee for Paquito and a medium latte for Lucia, they start by making awkward conversation, typical of those who are just getting acquainted, but gradually, their conversation grows more intimate. They share childhood experiences and stories about their respective families and friends. Paquito also tells her about his new friend, Mr. Frank. Lucia tells Paquito about Jeanette Norton, her five-year-old daughter from a failed marriage a few years ago. Paquito listens to Lucia and shows interest in her daughter, questioning about her schooling and hobbies, which Lucia answers with a very happy and proud tone. "You never said where you live, Lucia," Paquito asks, changing the subject.

"That's right, sorry. I don't live in New York, but in Pennsylvania. In a small city called Camp Hill—well, not exactly in the city but about thirty minutes from downtown. I'm taking a few days' vacation and staying at a good friend's house here in Staten Island—you know, the kind of vacation you take when you don't have enough money to go on a cruise or take an airplane to Paris."

Paquito laughs, then tells her more details about his family. He's comfortable enough to confide in Lucia about how his father mysteriously disappeared.

"But Paquito, what if that new friend of yours, Mr. Frank, is really your dad?"

At this point, Lucia has collected enough information about Paquito's father and his friend Mr. Frank, and she is curious. Such a question leaves Paquito stunned and suddenly nervous; that's not something he's considered.

"Forgive my indiscretion," Lucia says, "but as you said, your friend seems to be everywhere. You even said you resemble one another. Don't you ever wonder why he showed up all of a sudden and became your friend?"

Paquito refuses to think about it. He smiles, preferring to see Lucia's theory as a passing comment, a pointless point of view. Whatever it was, he doesn't want to spend time thinking about something that isn't true. Still, she's waiting for a response...

"Lucia, I've been a friend to Mr. Frank for some time already. My first encounter with him was not because I was looking for him or he was looking for me; it was a thing of destiny. Remember the rain I told you about, when Mr. Frank kindly invited me into his house? In addition, he knows about my family because I talked to him about them, including the disappearance of my dad. Don't you think he would have said something himself? Why would he hide something like that?"

Lucia nods in response without taking her eyes off Paquito. She seems surprised by his response. "Maybe I've gone too far with this matter. We barely know each other, and I've already touched on such a delicate theme."

"No, no!" Paquito hurries to say. "It's no problem, really. I'm touched that you care enough about my story to share your ideas. Your hopeful attitude is a beautiful thing."

Ready to move on from this subject, Paquito praises Lucia, telling her that her eyes are magical, that she is beautiful, and that her smile steals all his attention. Lucia likes the compliments and blushes.

The conversation takes shape and makes its way between formality and familiarity. They end the day in a happy and very fruitful way. Both keep in touch after that emotional late afternoon, and as days go by, the phone calls keep piling up, as does the desire growing between the two. After a few months, it is Paquito who is most serious and focused on their future. Lucia is three years older than Paquito—something that seems not to matter to Paquito. It feels right to be in a mature, reciprocal relationship. Now Paquito's aspirations and goals merge with love and passion for this girl. As their relationship grows stronger, the need to be together is more necessary every day—so much so that they have even talked about living together and, perhaps, getting married.

In the same room as always, without any variation in its surroundings or its eternal silence, Mr. Frank serves himself his usual tea made from eucalyptus and soursop leaves. Calm and concentrated on the whispers in his mind, he gets up from the chair and walks to the back of the house. He reaches the middle of the courtyard and stands still and stares at a stone headstone that looks many years old. His countenance hardens and becomes mournful. A tear falls from his eye as he remembers someone, who, under that pile of rocks, rests in their final shelter and last abode—obviously a beloved one.

That batch of stone is strong, although the cross is not properly set but inclined. It seems to have been improperly maintained based on the large amount of dust and dirt on it, which cover the scriptures carved there that would identify the deceased. He bows, and with that same gloom that has accompanied him all afternoon says, "So much philosophizing and preaching about the happy freedom that comes with the end of servitude and imprisonment to this damned body that will not let me be with you even one more time. Damn this mysterious border of flesh and bones that takes us away from the truth. How do you know if you are at the end or the prelude to a beginning?"

Sensibility snatches him. He then feels the need to dust off the headstone but stops and does not. Mr. Frank breathes deeply and instead turns around, drops the cloth in his hands, and walks back into the house. Emotional, he stands before the piece that is covered with a white mantle—the same one that aroused Paquito's curiosity.

"Hi."

Mr. Frank turns around, and there is Paquito entering the house.

"So good you're here." He invites him in and tells him to settle without any concern about how Paquito entered the house if he does not have a key. Rather, and without hesitation, he moves back into the yard and collects some eucalyptus and soursop leaves. Then he puts a small pot of water to heat on the stove, pours it, and finally, he passes a cup to the boy.

"How have you been, Mr. Frank? I haven't seen you for a while," Paquito says.

"Sitting here, as always, heating the seat, my young friend. Looking at life and the many things it gives us, the things that life itself, perhaps with aloofness, lets us savor—as you know." He pauses a few seconds, then adds, "I am worried about your situation. I feel what's going on, but I don't want to accept it either. Sometimes I suffer a lot, believe it or not."

It does not look like the boy likes what he said at all.

"I'm not sure why you're concerned, but I guess this is about Lucia. You know I am very careful with these things. I know you think I'm young, but I don't get carried away so easily with emotions."

The old man responds with a short smile.

"I want you to know I've had other girlfriends and love affairs with pretty women. But with Lucia, it's different. I've never felt an attraction like this before, Mr. Frank. You know that chemistry one feels with that special person. Besides, you don't even know Lucia—at least I don't think you do, though there are times when I wonder… I have a suspicion that you know something about her that I don't know. Is that so?"

Mr. Frank sighs and tilts his head morosely. "The heart tells us one thing and the mind another. Never underestimate family culture or behavior, boy. Sometimes, people feel the need to fake suffering and pain to get attention. Oh, some people, boy... You wouldn't be the first to follow the theory of chemistry, Paquito. Love is something beautiful—worthy, even—but when it is the main course, reality must at least be the dessert.

Failure to eat this diet could end with tremendous diarrhea, kid."

Mr. Frank wears a funny expression on his face. "It becomes difficult to see things for what they are when certain feelings get in the way, which is certainly human nature. It is the most natural failure of man. Or maybe it is nature that sometimes contrasts with the order of the modern man. That is, the interest and values of today's man go against the natural way of being. Well, what else can I say?"

In a low voice and with a small attitude, he says,

"Certainly that I know her."

He carries on: "People don't always agree, sometimes because they are bad or good. Sometimes, it is because they are one or the other. What I mean is, many times, it is not that people are bad or good, but instead they are different. They don't understand each other because they are like water and oil. The point is, we have to get together with people who resemble us. The greater the equality, the better the understanding and coexistence, because this is all that remains after the spark fades, boy."

The boy is not very impressed by the well-crafted words his wise friend has said. He glances around the house. "Forgive me, Mr. Frank, but of the many things we have talked about, I don't remember you saying anything about your family. I'm amazed that I don't even see a picture of a single family member anywhere, which is a normal thing to see in someone's house."

Although Paquito tried to ignore it, Lucia's observation regarding his relationship with the old man aroused his curiosity, and therefore, he's asking questions that could bring him closer to the truth.

Mr. Frank shows little concern and remains quiet and thoughtful. He stands with his hands away from the window and looks through it, like he is trying to find the horizon of the outside world. Paquito is also serene but looks closely at the old man. He feels ignored, and it arouses even more curiosity.

"Love, as I have commented, is strong and determined. You worry more about what Lucia has told you—a girl you just met not long ago—than what I've warned you about her." Mr. Frank looks straight at the boy. "Don't think I blame you for that, though."

Then he smiles and walks around Paquito. "Look, my son, you met her at a bar; it is not exactly a place where people of a certain level or of good families frequent."

Paquito quickly replies, "Oh no, Mr. Frank. She doesn't frequent that place as much as you might think. It was her first time, as it was for me too. You know, there are situations that can lead one anywhere."

"Paquito, there are situations that justify the actions of a man, but a girl is different."

"That's not how I see it, Mr. Frank. Believe me, I understand, but today, things are a little different than they were years ago."

"Let's see if I understand," Mr. Frank says. "Now you'll lecture me about today's women having the same rights and needs as men. That's where this is going, right?"

"I don't want you to feel offended, Mr. Frank, but really, times are very different now."

"Well, young friend, if I can assure you of anything, it is that I can see both ends of these times you're talking about, but can you? I lived that time day by day, night by night, situation by situation, just like I also live them today. What have you lived? Half as long?"

Now the old man looks directly into Paquito's eyes and approaches him face-to-face. He raises his voice and almost shouts, asking him, "Are you blind, boy? Don't you get the point yet? I am my life and yours—together! Maybe if you'd listen to me for a moment, I could save you from the ninety-nine failures of the one hundred attempts you will make in life! Do you have any idea of the difference between the youth and the elderly? What do you think they are? Some wrinkles instead of softer and smoother skin? A swollen belly from a flat one? The silver hair and some bald spots instead of a beautiful bushy mane? Or maybe you just think a young man is able to burst into running like a madman or jumping and taking a girl two or three times on a single day, uncontrollably and without thinking about consequences?"

The boy is speechless, as if afraid of adding anything else to fuel Mr. Frank's fire or giving the wrong answer. The old man falls silent, walks away, and takes seat.

"You must see reality, son. A man is different from a woman. That is a truth that should not go unnoticed by anyone. In a bar, you can find a female prostitute more easily than a male prostitute; that's another fact. A woman can be more easily raped by a man walking late in the dark streets than a man can be raped by a woman—another reality. For some psychological reason, the man tends to vent his sorrows by going out to have drinks. A woman, on the other hand, is known to have more control than the man in moments like that. It is a matter of things having their places. Neither is better than the other, but they are different—not only in the breech of the buttocks but also psychologically."

The old man adds, "If you think about all that I tell you and you also consider the kind of society we live in, of macho men and ignorance, I do not think you'll end up very content in that relationship. Don't forget what they say about a man when he meets a woman at the bar and they end up in court: *remember where I met you*."

Mr. Frank laughs mockingly, as if he is losing his mind. It seems he is talking to the wall and not to a friend visiting him. "You're not the only one who has entered that bar, nor is it the first time she has," he says, and the words cause even greater astonishment and disappointment in Paquito, who gets up from the chair. He feels feverish and uncomfortable. He turns around and walks toward the door to leave the house. He does not even say goodbye. It seems he prefers to move away so as not to release his tongue and offend the poor old man.

Mr. Frank, on the other hand, remains serene, as if nothing has happened—not even flinching. He is gone in his mind, and he shakes one of Paquito's hands, as if doing so with both would cause him to lose his concentration, which he doesn't want to let go. Under such concentration, he sees Paquito vanish into the bushes, but Mr. Frank remains there.

There has definitely been a special attraction between Paquito and Lucia since they first met. Paquito has become so devoted to her that his many aspirations and efforts toward enrichment, fame, and being a great businessman now remain in the background. It is his need to join Lucia that has prospered and created a very significant change in Paquito's life.

The girl is beautiful, but she lives far away in a small city about five hours from where Paquito lives. Manipulated by the strong emotions he feels for her, he sets out with the hope and possibility of better opportunities. After giving his mom a valid and reasonable explanation about his decision to leave her and get away, the big boy packs his luggage and starts the journey. It is an unknown and remote city, but the boy does not get pessimistic. There are plenty of happy moments full of excitement and emotion between Paquito and Lucia once they are together in the small town. Jeanette, Lucia's young daughter, also lives with the couple. Paquito has no complaints about the house where they live together. The house is big enough, with three bedrooms, one and a half restrooms, a spacious living room, a wooden porch, a small grassy yard, and a comfortable kitchen with a brand-new stove that the new couple bought with their savings just before moving in. It feels as if they really are meant for each other, when in fact, their arrangement is based on nothing more than physical attraction between them.

After a few months pass by and the outpouring of carnal desire gradually dissipates, Paquito becomes more concentrated on finding a new, better job. Lucia has a job that is not so badly paid, but Paquito, as a responsible man, is not satisfied with the little he earns and feels the need to contribute more and better the house. But he can't find the job he thinks he should be able to and could find so easily back in the city.

But this does not stop Paquito. The boy, longing for a higher degree of responsibility, ends up taking a job offered to him by a cousin of Lucia. The job is still below his capacity, and it pays half the salary he could make in his hometown. Moreover, the position has nothing to do with what he had studied. But it is time to be realistic, and so he pretends to be happy. The last thing he wants to do is bring sadness or discouragement to his life partner and his new home.

This whole situation has also forced Lucia to find a way to make a higher income. Having more knowledge of the area, she easily finds an opportunity to make more money than what she did.

The day comes when Mrs. Zoila, Lucia's mother, arrives at their home for vacation. She is originally from a small and backward town on the east coast of the Dominican Republic and travels to the US to visit her daughter and other relatives once in a while. She plans not just to stay a few weeks in the couple's home, but months. Mrs. Zoila looks a lot like Lucia physically but is sixty-five years old and moderately overweight, which already seems to be slightly perturbing her.

While this is a new experience in the house, Paquito, Lucia, and Jeannette enjoy the visit of Mrs. Zoila. They spent the first few days taking Mrs. Zoila to different places to shop and to dine in different restaurants. Mrs. Zoila, of course, is enchanted by all of the attention from the couple. As the days pass by, she starts to feel more and more comfortable and begins to reveal some of her bad manners typical of aged people raised in the countryside.

Mrs. Zoila keeps an eye on how everything operates within the house, and with all the "intelligence" in the world manipulates the minds of those more gullible—namely her daughter Lucia. This devoted Christian woman cannot miss Sunday church services and is unable to eat even a piece of bread without a prayer to heaven to thank God. And at night, before going to sleep, she must read verses of the Holy Bible, which is indispensable according to her principles and needed to nourish the soul and achieve God's forgiveness of our sins.

This whole situation restricts spending in the house, but it is not much trouble to Paquito, who has the best of intentions to please his partner however possible.

One evening, Paquito comes home from work and finds Mrs. Zoila complaining of a strong headache. He asks Mrs. Zoila if she needs any kind of medicine that would help to alleviate her suffering. The lady is silent, just shakes her head no, but continues showing the discomfort she feels by covering her face with her left arm and avoiding a direct eye contact with Paquito, which increases his concern. Her expression of displeasure increases, and that is when Paquito makes a decision: he must take her to the hospital.

He assists her to the car and at the same time grabs his cell phone and tells Lucia about the situation with her mother. She agrees to leave work and meet them at the hospital. He runs to Jeanette's bedroom. She is playing with a doll, but he tells her to put a jacket on and also shoes. So, she does so with Paquito's help, and the three drive to the hospital. When they arrive, Paquito helps Lucia's mother into the hospital emergency room, always holding her by the arm but also holding Lucia's daughter with his other hand. They are received by a nurse who sits at a small desk in the waiting room. She takes Mrs. Zoila's blood pressure and examines her eyes.

"Please, sit and wait," she tells them.

Paquito relaxes, realizing the matter is not as urgent as he thought. He waits for a few minutes, and soon, a nurse calls Mrs. Zoila to a window, where she receives medication. Paquito is confused, because what was supposed to be an emergency does not appear to be one at all. He feels uneasy and suspicious, but at the same time, he is glad to know that Lucia's mother is not as ill as she seemed.

But again, a few days later, the boy encounters the same medical emergency and hurries to take Lucia's mother to the hospital as he did the first time. In the end, the diagnosis is the same, and the embarrassed attitude of Lucia is not much different, though more reserved. Paquito, on the other hand, feels frustrated and uncomfortable.

Over time, as similar situations arise, Paquito comes to understand his beloved's family better and that this kind of behavior is a family pattern. When there is a family gathering, they partake in conversations about illnesses, prescriptions, and any suffering that afflicts them, and almost always, there is at least one of them with serious health problems.

Well, this family has serious problems, he thinks. Paquito recalls some comments that his friend Mr. Frank made about those who make drama to get the attention of others and to inspire pity and ruin others' peace when they don't have a more interesting topic to talk about. He said it is a sweet feeling that that kind of person gets from feeling sick. It can't be an easy thing to play such a game, Paquito thinks, and he begins to feel mocked. It becomes clear that he cannot continue to endure such ridiculous charades that, sooner or later, will damage the home environment.

About five months pass, and Mrs. Zoila has not left the house yet. Like any couple, Paquito and Lucia have their differences, and sometimes, they even argue over trivial things. But the discussions that so far have been kept between the two now include the intervention of Lucia's mother, who plays the role of a referee. With a direct and eager advocate, Lucia seems emboldened to not just criticize Paquito, but put a lot of pressure on him. Then there is Lucia's daughter, Jeanette, who is so young she can't do anything but cry during these kinds of altercations in the house. Love is still there between Paquito and Lucia, but the relationship is now breaking apart, and there is not much happening in the bedroom that, just a year before, saw so much of love and caring.

But the tense hours would pass, and their nerves would gradually return to their place before the end to a difficult day came. It is one of those nights, made up of quiet and sparkling stars. The boy walks toward his bedroom, then lies on his bed with his head on the pillow. He feels tired and tries to sleep, looking outside through the window that is next to the bed. He concentrates on the sky and those quiet, bright stars, when out of nowhere, a delineated image interrupts him. It is the face of Mr. Frank. Because of this vision, Paquito again remembers his old friend's advice, but he refuses to get lost in those inopportune thoughts. He blinks a few times, slips between the sheets, and falls into a deep sleep.

Paquito finds himself in the middle of a garden full of beautiful and exotic flowers, in the center of a huge green field. On its summit, a vast blue sky stretches, and beautiful puffs of very white clouds mysteriously delineate the face of his friend Mr. Frank.

Beautifully arranged in a white dress made from fine cotton that falls to the knees, Lucia wears a wide-brimmed English-style hat the color of tropical blue. It sits distinctly on her shiny black hair, and she dazzles within this chimera painting. Bewitched by her female beauty,

Paquito approaches, and they walk together across the edge of a majestic lake.

There is a long white blanket that extends over the grass, and on it are two glasses of champagne that complement the paradise scenario. Two beautiful angels suspended in the air accompany the scene with the beautiful melody of their harps.

Lucia looks more beautiful than ever, and Paquito sees her the way he did in those early days. He is full of love and desire to possess her and does not take his eyes off her. She also looks at him and thinks of nothing more than being able to touch him, and so she does so. As they shed their clothes with closed eyes, they kiss and embrace. Passion consumes the desire they have been feeling for a little while. With sweat and relief, both relax between sighs and sleepy, happy looks.

It is then that Paquito notices Lucia's mother, who does not wear that hateful expression or undesirable look she normally has; to the contrary, she wears a candid smile of happiness and fulfillment at seeing her daughter so pleased between the arms of her companion. Paquito feels the exaltation of the complicated lady, and it makes him feel so comfortable and satisfied. Everything is harmonious in that panorama. They are the perfect four: Lucia, Mrs. Zoila, Mr. Frank, and Paquito. Not only is Paquito's body fulfilled from the pleasure of sex, but also his mind is enriched and his soul relishes in peace. It is a peak state of well-being.

But then he wakes up. A loud noise from the kitchen jars him, jerking him from the middle of that beautiful and romantic dream. He hurries to see what's occurring. He meets Lucia and his mother-in-law, who are discussing the unpleasant situation in the house. Paquito realizes that the main problem is none other than him. He, still off-center and confused from the pleasant dream, tries to talk to Mrs. Zoila and defend himself. She cuts him off and asks him if he intends to take any action, demanding that he be responsible and take better care of her daughter. She insists that her daughter deserves a better life. Paquito responds the best way he can, but Lucia's mother keeps going, calling him immature, saying he does not deserve Lucia's love.

It is clear that Mrs. Zoila believes Paquito should work harder and provide a better life for his new family, and it seems both women see him as a man who was incompetent and lazy. The weight of the situation settles on Paquito. He is aware that Mrs. Zoila is from the outskirts of the city, where people have a different way of seeing things, and that for that reason, he is not exactly the type of man who could meet this family's expectations.

Paquito suffers a heartbreaking moment, realizing it does not matter what he says, Mrs. Zoila will not listen to him. He turns and looks to Lucia for support, but instead, she backs away and ignores him while Mrs. Zoila shouts, eating him alive with her criticisms. It is clear Lucia is not on his side, and her attitude corroborates most of the things her mother is saying—that she needs a more productive man.

"Well then, it makes no sense to continue talking about this," Paquito says with the frustration that now overwhelms him. He feels lonely with these people, and his body is cold from the betrayal. He prefers not to add anything else. He turns around and goes back to his room while Lucia's mother— like a red-bellied piranha in attack mode—walks after him and continues to shout unpleasant and offensive words at him.

Paquito refuses to stoop to her level. The whole situation makes him understand that he has to go—not because of the pain he feels now, but because of the disappointment, which is poison to his noble soul. To leave Lucia, a woman he still loves, will not be an easy thing to do, but she does not belong to him anymore but rather to her mommy. There is nothing more to think about it, and so Paquito starts packing his things. While he does, Lucia asks him not to go, begging him to speak to her first and before leaving. She seems surprised; perhaps she did not expect Paquito to take her so seriously and decide to leave home. Paquito remains silent, knowing that Lucia does not really understand the reason he has to leave. She cannot imagine the shame and humiliation that has resulted from the scene with her mother. She cannot understand the betrayal and lack of control Paquito feels now.

Suitcase in hand, Paquito moves to leave the house immediately. Lucia is in tears. Lucia's mother, on the other hand, sits on the couch with her eyes closed, pretending to be asleep, because the last thing she wants to do is say something that might grab Paquito and change his mind to stay. Regardless, staying in such embarrassing circumstances is something the boy will not do, and Paquito leaves the house and heads back to his mother's place.

There is still communication between Paquito and Lucia over the phone for a time after the whole terrible breakup takes place. They try to understand each other and solve things, but the relationship is already deeply damaged, and in the end, they simply reach an agreement about selling the house and the subsequent distribution of the money.

Paquito has cried and mourned the end of his relationship with his great love. He wants to go out and talk to someone, to even tell strangers about his grief and find some kind of comfort in doing so, but he refrains. He sees the sad face of an old friend he hasn't seen in a while and hears him say, "These are times when the path is best navigated by the soul, without the vices of the flesh, my young friend."

He listens and sees in his mind the face of his old friend Mr. Frank. Paquito starts walking quickly toward this friend's house. He needs to talk and understands that someone with Mr. Frank's long life experience is the best option.

"It is a pleasure to see you. You don't know just what a pleasure it is," Mr. Frank says when the boy enters. "I look at your face, and I think I can even read your eyes. Tell me, boy, what's wrong with you?"

Delighted at these words, Paquito opens up and tells Mr. Frank about the things that torment him. The old man listens calmly, and when he sees how relieved the boy feels, he stays quiet as well.

"Mr. Frank, I want to thank you for the patience you have had with me. A person like me does not usually reach these extremes. I think what I must do is stay focused on my goals." He observes a huge sketch that Mr. Frank has hanging on one of the walls.

"Do you want to ask something, little friend?"

Mr. Frank says, his eyes on the sketch.

"This is another interesting one, Mr. Frank." Paquito points. "I can even tell the firmness with which you used the pencil for this drawing."

"Good observation for a rookie, Paquito. I didn't want to interrupt the drawing by choosing colors. I couldn't waste time on secondary things. My mom was the greatest thing in my life. It was not easy for me when she left—and so suddenly too. Without any warning, the will of God pulled her from me."

It's clear Mr. Frank is very hurt. "Your love is that simple, I imagine. And in the long run, as you know, you have to understand that it works strangely." He looks at Paquito face-to-face. The movements of his lips express a forced joy, even complacency. "When she died, I was thirty years old. A long time ago, right? At that age, I thought I was a very mature man fit to face any situation, and you are still even younger than what I was then. I'm sorry to say, her death made me understand that age in the soul and love does not exist, and there is not an age limit on pain so deep and strong like that. As anyone in my situation, I tried to comply with the protocol of the times—you know, people came to give condolences and told me to be strong. So many silly things. Of course, some people really mean what they say and say it with such sincerity, and that is a true friend. But remember, if there is something important in this short life, it is freedom, to be free. Keep in mind that we are part of this society, which is attached to the right to be free, so if you feel like crying, well...nothing can be more human than that. You must open yourself completely and enjoy the relief and the freedom to be able to do it."

He turns and looks at the drawing again. "There in those shadows was where I took refuge from the immense pain. That's why I used such black charcoal."

As Mr. Frank grieves, Paquito acknowledges his feelings, then talks about life and his art.

"Thank you, boy. It's been a long time already, of course, but it is not forgotten. You even feel guilty when you start forgetting them."

"Haven't you thought about framing it?" Paquito gestures to the drawing that is still unframed. The old man wears a soft smile. "The drawing goes with what I just told you, Paquito. I don't know if you understand. Framing is the last thing you do to a painting; you know that, boy. This one is not finished yet, because the love and pain are still there."

Silence falls between them, but the soft whistle of the wind can be heard coming and going from the branches of the trees that surround the small house.

"It's a good time for tea," Mr. Frank says. He moves to the patio to pick some leaves for his favorite drink. Then he comes back into the small kitchen, and there he takes a pot, small and burned a dark color from how old it is and how much fire has been lit beneath it. It is the one he always uses to heat things, like soups or tea. The old man turns on the stove and stands there. While waiting, he tilts his head and looks through the window. There is nothing new; it is the same landscape as always, but he is always looking for a new meaning, a reason to enjoy the simple act of living. He turns off the stove.

"With a few more years, or rather, with a little

more wisdom, you could be greatly happy with a cup of hot tea in your hands." He passes the second cup of tea to Paquito. "But be careful, boy; it is very hot, like so many things, right? Tea is good but must be given the necessary time to cool off, and then it must be imbibed slowly so it does not burn." Again, the old man smiles.

"I cannot deny that you are often quite right in the things you say, Mr. Frank. And I know I'm much younger than you are and that you have had many more experiences than me. But I think a person's way of life depends on their individual experiences."

"You're very right, my friend. The fruits of your life are the results of that which is your life. That's the point I've always wanted you to see. Every conclusion in life leads you to see what Paquito really is, Paquito—good things and bad things. It is up to you what you are going to choose, and what's chosen today might be the happiness of tomorrow."

"So, does happiness exist?

Mr. Frank laughs. "I did not expect that question, but as long as you accompany it with nature—or Mother Nature, as we call it sometimes." "Excuse me, Mr. Frank," Paquito interrupts, "but you always are so deep and confusing."

"I prefer to leave it half-told instead of missing another visit from you in the future."

"How is that?"

"Whatever I say could go against your principles. At your age, you have aspirations and don't go along with conformism. In many cases, the state of resignation gives you peace and even happiness; it takes the stress away."

"But, Mr. Frank, without hard work and stress, you often don't get anything in life, let alone achieve your goals."

"Of course, many times you don't achieve your goal—or success, as you say—but you get to other places and different situations. Well, maybe you don't remember, but we've already touched on this topic before." Mr. Frank changes to another subject: "Don't you want something to eat?"

He gets up from the chair and walks toward the kitchen. "Cooking is something you should do from time to time. It is a tremendous therapy." Mr. Frank takes another sip of tea and gives a discreet smile. "Sometimes we talk too much, don't we? At your age—I mean, when you are young— you have all the time in the world to deal with whatever case comes up, and these things are commonly women."

He bends down into the aged refrigerator and grabs some onions, garlic, and peppers.

"If you can enjoy cooking rather than going to a restaurant, you have full awareness of what you are eating. Even more so when you know just how to prepare it—at least a basic knowledge of how to cook and what ingredients you have to add. It may sound like nonsense to you, but age makes you appreciate simple things like that. Watch..." Mr. Frank gestures to the countertop.

"I am aware that I am including exactly one onion, two heads of garlic, and green Italian peppers. But I also know that they are fresh and organic, healthy, since I planted them myself here in my yard. Do you see why I suggest being aware of what you are consuming? Because it also applies to the things you drink."

"But that is not always the case, Mr. Frank. We must also give credit to the advances that have been made in the quality of our food. Milk pasteurization is an example of that; thanks to it, we avoid diseases."

"There have always been advances, boy, of course, and that of the milk has been one of the most important. But ask yourself if there have been more advances or damage that we have suffered? Once you answer that question, we enter into another field—a simple one."

He adds, "If you look, you will see many inventions that are now everywhere, such as machines in hospitals that are used to detect supposed diseases and even medicines that are prescribed for ailments and diseases.

Often, they are important and serve, but on many occasions, we exaggerate their use and application and rely on them too heavily. They diagnose things the body itself can warn you about. For example, something you eat or drink that is bad or does not suit you. We and even animals can smell things before ingesting them. And if that isn't warning enough, our sense of taste can tell us whether or not something should be ingested."

"But Mr. Frank, telling humans to simply smell their food before eating it to determine if it is spoiled is bad education."

The old man laughs out loud. "You can see how far we go that he prefers to risk his health and even his life before giving the impression of bad manners or of going against protocol in public." He laughs again, then steeps a new cup of tea. "The tea is much better when hot." Mr. Frank nods while enjoying a fresh sip. "Hasn't it happened to you that you don't feel hungry until you look at the food? Specifically, your favorite kind of food."

Paquito acknowledges that this is true.

"The truth is that I could not give you an exact answer as to why that is. Remember, I am no scholar or scientist, but in my case, I've been around a while. When it comes to our bodies, it happens even with sugar, which is not so healthy. We see a piece of chocolate and feel like eating it because the body is in need of that kind of energy. Fever and vomiting are other ways the body defends itself against bad and poisoned things. One forces you to lie in bed and rest, and the other makes you expel the bad things by mouth." He smiles. "And I'm crazy with garlic, Paquito."

He slices a couple of the cloves of garlic. "Whoever enjoys a good kitchen also finds the best excuse to fill it with good conversation."

Mr. Frank turns around to face the door, takes a few slow steps, and bends over, taking Paquito's teacup from the center of the table. It feels cold and heavier than his, but he doesn't ask why Paquito hasn't drank much of his tea. He smiles again and inhales deeply, throwing his chest out, seeking out with his nose the pleasant aroma of his cooking that comes from the kitchen.

"From the way you enjoy the aroma of food, I think you can really be happy with anything, Mr. Frank."

Mr. Frank turns to the door again and smiles at Paquito. "If you don't despair, you will eat good and healthy, my friend."

"I'm fine, Mr. Frank. I'm not that hungry."

"Don't worry. It's not going to be that long that you have to wait—something like half an hour. Everything is already covered. You just have to wait for it to cook slowly over low heat..." Once more, he exhibits his classic smile. "Remember?"

"I think I do know what you mean," Paquito says. "Things take whatever time is necessary to get them right. Is that it?"

"That's more or less what I mean, boy. Mankind's mind is something you need to know. It is good that you remember things when I prompt you. With my comment, I encouraged your memory, and the more your mind turns to your memory, the more profoundly you can dig into it and access stories very old and almost forgotten. Then you can store them away for the next time you need them."

Mr. Frank pauses before continuing. "Well, friend of mind, the truth is that I want to tell you something, almost out of obligation. I want to tell you something about my life. It is one of those many experiences of mine…"

He seems very concentrated now. He takes a short breath. "It was a night of so much torment. It was late at night already, but I didn't even think about throwing myself in bed and trying to sleep, so I went to a restaurant. Sometimes, to make room for the distressed soul, the best you can do is go somewhere—somewhere you can have a few drinks and maybe, with some luck, meet someone you can talk to who will listen. Without thinking twice, I ordered a whiskey, pure and without ice. The first sip burned my throat all the way through."

"Sounds like my experience, Mr. Frank. Of course, I imagine you have lived moments like this on many occasions."

"I have seen so many beautiful sunsets, but none are like the one you can enter and sweeten your most bitter realities and needs." He turns to the boy. "Nothing like a woman, Paquito."

When Paquito doesn't respond, he continues telling his story. "It was not until the second drink that I noticed that wayward princess in the bar. Of course, *wayward* is how I describe her now that I am fully aware of what she really was. But, in the moment, I saw her as a princess: sexy, elegant, full of life. Well, then we met and fell in love. We were crazy about each other, dated for some time, and eventually got married."

"That part doesn't look to be the case anymore..." Paquito says.

"She had two daughters despite her young age. One of them had gone with her father when she was very young. This man had promised her everything. He had even paid for her college, but that didn't prosper at all. She did not even make it through the first semester. The other daughter was even younger, thirteen years old, and still lived with my princess when I married her."

Paquito's eyes open wide. "Really?" he asks in surprise. "I think I see a coincidence now."

"What coincidence, son?"

"I have not told you this, but Lucia had another relationship before me, when she was much younger, and she has a young daughter with that ex-husband."

Mr. Frank nods but does not acknowledge this news. "In moments like that, at a young age, the heart overcomes the brain. So with this girl I am telling you about, I never saw any problems coming. It was all pleasure, sex, lots of love, and beautiful, nice words; there were plenty of flowers and romantic walks. But over time, those emotions faded, and of course, we had to break up. And as if it weren't painful enough just to separate, our relationship ended in me being accused of abusing her child."

Mr. Frank searches Paquito's face, then peeks at his own cup of tea. "My tea has cooled, but it's not as cold as whiskey is."

He goes to the kitchen to check out the cooked food. He uncovers the two pots on the stove and peeks in, then takes the spoon and stirs. He also takes a sip to taste how the cooking is coming along. With a satisfied expression on his face, he again covers the cauldron and sits down.

"Can you imagine something like it? Some women do not know how to lose." Mr. Frank adds, "The old men in the time of my ancestors, those people in the country where my parents were from, used to say a woman is chosen like a cow… by their race." Just like that, Mr. Frank expresses his racist side. "I suffered so much because of that mess I got into. I still remember that poor young girl, full of viciousness and bad habits—not to mention her mother…always blundering."

"Her daughter was vicious?"

"She had a drug addiction, Paquito. Just imagine… That stuff brings so much trouble. Two pesos to buy a bit of that shit. I don't know how I never noticed. At eighteen years of age, she didn't have any tattoos on top, but apparently, she had them on the rest of her body."

"There are very bad people, Mr. Frank."

"It may be, Paquito, but maybe the girl was just the victim of the same old story, a hard life she was not strong enough to deal with."

"That's not how I see it, Mr. Frank. If we make excuses for everyone's bad behavior, we will end up believing that no one is bad."

"It's a good point, kid. What we have to think about is how to solve a problem like that. It happens in very stable, experienced, developed countries, whose policies include many good social programs of assistance and support, which help people without jobs and prevent them from ending up doing improper things, such as stealing. Sadly, they need these programs to eat, dress, and pay their rent. Have you heard of Maximilien de Robespierre?"

Paquito shakes his head.

"If I tell you how this philosopher thought, surely you will not agree with him. He makes the case that very bad people—terrorists and criminals—have noble souls but have been very hurt or abused. These people can only react to a situation one of two ways: good or bad. They reach a point when their tolerance can no longer endure and explode, and at that point, they don't give a damn about their fate. It's like thinking you have nothing to lose, even when your dignity is at stake. This French man, unlike many others of his time, was the only one who addressed the problem of terrorists from a spiritual point of view. He tried to understand their psychological situation and see deep inside them. In that, I even resemble Velázquez, the Spanish painter. In his artwork *Juan de Pareja*, they say Velázquez was the first to paint the soul in the eyes of a person in an oil painting." "Sure, Mr. Frank. Who would overlook a great painter like him? I have read a lot about him. But I understand the point… It must be hard for people who have gone through problems and difficulties, but this doesn't justify killing someone. Many innocents that have nothing to do with anything and even children have suffered as a result of these damaged people."

"Sure, Paquito, I wouldn't agree any less. But it would be even better if a solution could be found to prevent these atrocities. As that great Mexican liberator said once, 'Respect of the rights of others is peace.'" The old man adds, "It scares me to see the inside of those who are labeled as bad people."

A very deep silence returns and reigns there in the modest and humid kitchen. The whistling of the gentle wind caresses the windows, resulting in yellowish curtains waving elegantly at them.

"The more you age, the more understanding and forgiving you become. It is best not to resent or hate. I suffered that kind of betrayal," he says, returning to the subject of his former partner and her daughter. "The truth is that many times, I felt like setting them all on fire—even the mother-in- law, the architect of all the hell in that house. They are things you start to see more clearly as time goes by, boy. When you give more attention to your mental and spiritual health than to anything material, you have less problems."

He throws a glance at Paquito. "And I hope I don't offend you with that. It's just that I know how you think." Mr. Frank gets up from the chair again and moves toward the kitchen. "It is time to avoid issues that ruin moments as pleasant as this. I think the cooking is done. I don't know if you're hungry, but I need to eat something. And believe me, my friend, I will enjoy every bite of these vegetables and boiled little meats, cooked with my hands and with my pure imagination."

Mr. Frank uncovers the pots and serves food onto two old dishes made of porcelain. He spreads a tablecloth and gets some utensils as well as a couple of glasses and sets the table for two. "Feel at home, Paquito. It may not be the tastiest food that has ever been made, but it is good and healthy."

Mr. Frank takes a seat at one end of the small but well-made oak table and starts eating. He observes Paquito and swears the boy enjoys every spoonful that he puts into his mouth.

"I think what you said about this French philosopher seems much the same style as Sigmund Freud. Though I don't think he was a Frenchman," Paquito says.

"I think he was an Austrian, Paquito. And what did Freud say that you relate him to Robespierre?" "Well, I don't remember exactly his words, but it was something regarding a person's frustrations and anger that they never let out. When people who never externalized these feelings get to unburden themselves, they do so in the worst ways." Paquito pauses to put another spoonful into his mouth. "I'm referring to a person who gets angry about something but keeps it inside and doesn't let off steam."

"I understand, boy. How is the food?"

"Oh, it's very rich, Mr. Frank. Forgive me for not saying anything about. It is very tasty. You are a great cook, Mr. Frank. I was distracted by our line of conversation, but of course, I like it. You are a real chef!"

"In one way or another, every thinking being observes what others cannot see. We all have the same mind, but not all of us organize or develop it in the same way. Our society encourages us to think a certain way based on what suits the government or country. It's like training people to be a part of the system."

"Yes, but that makes sense, right?"

The old man simply nods. "But you have to tend to and maintain your priorities, my friend." He puts the last full spoon in his mouth. "The kind of people that Mr. Freud refers to are similar to those I have spoken about—the people who endure until the day that they can no longer handle it and explode. There are those who don't know how to deal with violence, Paquito. It may not be an exact example, but imagine a person who doesn't know how to swim and suddenly falls into deep water. Does he despair trying to stay on the surface? Does he avoid drowning? At this moment, he will resort to action without any reason."

Paquito is mute while he takes his plate and puts it on the counter. He smiles. "Well, Mr. Frank, I will be going now."

The old man approaches him and shakes his hands. It is the end of a day and a long conversation between the two, a very productive one. Paquito leaves Mr. Frank alone. It's a very dark night, and Mr. Frank has little to do but go to bed—with a smile on his face, of course.

Two nights and one morning after Paquito returned to Mrs. Rosa's place after visiting Mr.

Frank, the old man, sits calmly in the gallery of his house. On his lap, he holds a book, which he looks at more than he reads, reading the same line repeatedly. He sobs slightly, lost in a private memory with pain in his eyes. Mr. Frank closes the book and raises his head. He looks at the sky and mumbles, "This is my life, my reality. It is my only way. What will happen to me?"

He closes his eyes and breathes air in deeply, looking forward to that bit of pure oxygen that is already in short supply.

"I want to go to sleep, but time does not let me. Who am I to decide? Or maybe I can? But why should I do so? Crying is not a sin, nor is feeling or showing sorrow for the dead. That's part of life, and so is time. The years go by and give you old age and subtract your youth. But aging means more time, more life, not less. Your life is as long as your old age. Your life has the same dimension as your past. It is not only your body; it is also your mind, your memory, and your experiences that make you wiser. That wisdom is the sum of living the past, the present, and to some extent, the future. The younger you are, the less you can see. Age determines the eyes of the soul."

There Mr. Frank releases the inspiration that has cornered him and goes out for a walk.

Interruptions to routine can spoil the morning, and this is of significance to Paquito and even more to Mr. Frank, who sees the boy approaching again. Paquito interrupts the walk Mr. Frank just started, but it is, nonetheless, a joyful moment. The visit of such a special friend is a pleasant encounter no matter the circumstances. They both enter the house and sit in the living room. After exchanging salutations, the boy tells Mr. Frank about his new pet and shows him a photo of it.

The old man observes the picture, then, though irrelevant, says, "There is nothing more dangerous than ignorance."

"Sure, Mr. Frank."

"It is more dangerous than hatred or any enemy of yours, no matter how great the desire of that enemy to harm you. Ignorance can get you in tremendous trouble, my boy. It can even kill you. Let's see if you understand me… With an enemy, there is obvious dislike and distrust, but someone you love and have confidence in has easier access to you."

"Well, I'm not so sure about that, Mr. Frank. Imagine, the Bible talks a lot about that and speaks of sin and hatred as the greatest flaws of humanity."

"My son, people talk so much about the Bible and rely on it to philosophize, theorize, and even justify the many things we do and what happens to us. Sure, the Bible says it all and very accurately, but how many really understand it is a different matter. It is the reason you see so many different churches; there are multiple interpretations of it." He pauses. "Anyway, back to ignorance, which is the most dangerous of all our defects…"

Paquito shakes his head. "Sometimes I hear you speak, and it gives me the feeling that you are a very noble and sensitive man at heart. As with all people who care about other living beings, the only thing missing is an animal. I mean, you live alone, and you're not the first person I've seen living like this, but other people usually have a pet—a cat or dog or at least a parakeet or parrot to serve as company."

"I don't have them, it's true, but you have seen many little birds fly near here and perch nearby, right?"

"Well, yes."

"I prefer to love what's around me, including the animals and birds."

"Yes, I know, Mr. Frank. Of course they should be taken care of. But anyway, in those places where pets are sold, they teach you how to take care of the animals so you are prepared."

Mr. Frank ignores him. "They sometimes have the same feelings that human beings have, and they also feel pain if you hurt them. That is why I prefer to take care of them by respecting their freedom. You see so many people who have caged birds and still enjoy it. They are beautiful, eat special things, and can be trained, but I wonder if you notice that in most cases, these birds have clipped wings. If not abuse, then what is that? For those little birds, their wings are the same as our legs, except they have no chance to have a wheelchair to help.

"This is why I have been talking about ignorance. It can be seen anywhere, all the time— mothers, fathers, and friends hurting their own children or relatives by not educating them. So many poisoning accidents—you've seen it, right?"

"Yes."

"Well, ignorance extends that much. If I care about a little bird, why would I eliminate their right to go and be wherever and whenever they please? Why would anyone keep a bird in a cage for entertainment? Or tie a dog on a leash? So many people everywhere have pets. They even go to bed with them believing that they are doing good by treating them as if they were a human being when they are not, and maybe those poor, innocent animals would not even want to be, but they can't complain because they can't talk, and so they tolerate it out of love. In many cases, my friend, it is not love that you are giving them; it is unconscious selfishness."

"I still remember the painting, Mr. Frank—the one with the tree and the little bird on the branch. There we go, right? This is what you mean with the painting. This is the message."

And the old man grants him a fine smile.

Paquito enters his place. His mom sits on a stool near the kitchen. She is sorting some papers on the kitchen table but looks up at Paquito as he walks through the room without saying anything. "And you, which mosquito has stung you?" she asks him while walking after him to his room. "Oh, Mom, here you come again with your weird language and idiomatic phrases! It's nothing." "Well, I'm your mom, and I know when something is bothering you. Tell me—problems with Lucia?"

"I don't know if any of it is really her fault... Sometimes I feel like—like I'm a fool." He waves away his mom's response. "It is true, Mom. It feels like, somehow, things have been hidden from me, and I'm tired of it. I think of Dad more than you imagine. It's not normal. People die; they are properly buried; or maybe they move away or abandon their house and family or get divorce... But to never again hear from your loving father? It doesn't make any sense."

Mrs. Rosa feels the frustration that has suddenly invaded her son in her soul. She looks at Paquito, worried.

"You really never knew anything? No one has even told us if there is any reasonable possibility? You never found out?" he asks.

Mrs. Rosa feels the distress of a boy who now is more mature, conscious, and therefore, curious. She takes a seat next to her son and tries to explain in the best way she can about the effort that was made when his father vanished. She tells him when she called the police and also how some of her relatives, neighbors, and close friends participated in the search.

She goes on with more details and tells Paquito about the morning when she saw his father last. “It was early in the morning, and your father finished his breakfast and had a cup of black coffee, as he would every morning. Then he left to take the metro that would take him to the work site. He always called me on his break, usually at one o’clock. Everything was normal. It was not until the clock struck 5:30 p.m. that I started to worry, since he was always home by 5:00 p.m. or five minutes after if he had to stop to get something from the grocery store on his way here. But he never came…even after a whole night passed.”

Mrs. Rosa cries. Paquito is sad and looks at her with sorrow.

“You don’t know how much I suffered, my son. A few days of desperation and crying were not enough to mitigate the sadness and despair that that time brought down on me. I cried every night when I went to bed. We looked for your dad for a very long time, and nothing. It was not only the affection and love that we had for him, but also the need; I was staying with you and out of work. By then, he was the only family support, and we had to pay our rent. He’d also financed a lot that year with the idea of fixing up a small, old house. All that in addition to the things we had to buy every day, of course.”

Now Paquito feels guilty for having made such a comment and, more than anything, for leading his mother to recount these bad memories. "I understand, Mom. Forgive my attitude. It's just that the earth could not have swallowed him whole. Dead or alive, he has to be somewhere. I'm not going to give up that easily."

"I understand, Paquito, and I know that you are old enough to feel the way you do, but I don't want you to get your hopes up. There are times in life when you have to accept the defeats and leave things as they are. We have to be realistic and move forward."

"Mom..."

"Tell me, Paquito."

"Do you remember my friend from the park?

The old man I told you I found so mysterious?"

Mrs. Rosa smiles slightly but tries to hide it as she imagines what is going through her young boy's mind. "Yes, Paquito, I remember."

Paquito falls silent now. He doesn't feel confident enough to share his theory, worried that his mother will see him as a fool boy. After a pause, he finally asks his mom, "Do you remember if Dad had a favorite pastime?"

"Your dad was an intelligent man despite never reaching college. Imagine, he had just completed high school there in the Dominican Republic and then went straight into the Navy at just sixteen. He was enlisted for a few years and got some promotions, but nothing else of much importance, actually. But he was always noticed and had social inclinations. He always wanted to read and learn, which he did in his free time. He liked art."

"To paint?" Paquito can't help but ask. As he patiently awaits a response, he feels something akin to fear.

"He liked paintings very much and boasted that he understood the feelings and inspirations of European painters. He talked so eloquently when referring to those things. But what he enjoyed the most was reading and philosophy." She smiles. "He didn't get along with religious people at all, and the truth is that very often, he drove me nuts with his ideas about freedom, society, and other things like that."

Paquito listens to his mother's words and feels a tremendous cold settling into his bones. Everything seems to connect. He can't help but compare Mr. Frank with the things his mother has said about his dad.

"But Mom, all of that kind of matches my friend. He likes to paint and talk about all those things: philosophy, nature, a painting inspired by freedom. There is a painting of a tree with a little bird that has no wings; he says it is one of his favorites."

Although Mrs. Rosa has tried to put any and all hope that this friend of Paquito's could be her husband aside, she considers what he says, remaining calm and a bit confused. She is afraid to respond and give Paquito any ideas or false hope. "Painting is something that many people like, Paquito. How old is this friend of yours?"

"I don't know. I never asked. He looks about seventy years old or more. He is about my height, with pale skin like me and gray hair; that's the best I can describe him. He also has a long gray beard, which covers part of his face and hides his wrinkles."

Mrs. Rosa looks calmer now and makes a suggestion. She, like Paquito, is curious, but wants to be discreet about it. "I don't know, Paquito. Maybe if you visit him again and have a look around… Haven't you seen any clues, like a family photograph, maybe? Hasn't he told you where he was born or if he ever had a family?"

"He doesn't have any pictures, at least not in the living room. And we haven't talked much about the past." He jumps. "Wait! How distracted I've been! It's as if I haven't spoken to him much at all—what a rare way to make a friendship. He already knows so much about me—almost everything, even what I haven't told him. And how does he know about Lucia? He never answered that either."

With a very slow tone, Mrs. Rosa makes a proposal: "Paquito, this is what we're going to do, but first, I will ask you not to get excited or get your hopes up. In the end, I am sure that Mr. Frank is just a friend and nothing else, a friend who looks a bit like your dad. We have to be realistic. With him living so close, the three of us would have realized this connection sometime earlier. It's been so long. As I've always told you, your father was a family man, a loyal man, and the last thing he would have done would have been to abandon us. If Mr. Frank was your father, the first thing he would have done when he met you would have been to find out about you and your family and rebuild that relationship. But the next time you visit Mr. Frank, with discretion, look for anything that is related to your father, like a photograph or piece of paper with his writing and things like it".

After talking with his mom, Paquito feels more at ease and especially much more hopeful. His phone rings; it's Lucia. That call from her changes the whole picture. Now he smiles, almost forgetting everything related to Mr. Frank, while his mother goes to tend the house until the day ends.

Standing between the living room and the kitchen, a thoughtful Mr. Frank looks up at the front door and sees his only company.

"Good to see you this evening, boy. Here I am, still trying to understand so many things that seem strange or silly to me."

"Always philosophizing, Mr. Frank," answers Paquito. "Maybe getting out somewhere or visiting a friend would be nice. Have you ever thought about that?" As Paquito makes this suggestion, he peeks around the living room, remembering his conversation with Mrs. Rosa about Mr. Frank. Considering his similarities with Paquito's father who disappeared, Paquito looks for any evidence. "I have lived so many years that I do not think

I have anything left to think, boy. Over time, you learn endless things, you meet people. I'm one of those people too, so I try not to judge anyone. But it seems we human beings can be sheep and wolf at the same time. In almost everyone, however good they are, there is always something wrong in them and vice versa."

The old man turns his gaze to one of the paintings that are hanging there and smiles. Again, Paquito looks around discreetly and spots something in one of the corners. He is not sure what it is, but he's interested in getting a better look at it and fixes his eyes on it.

"It is there where many of these brushstrokes over the canvas you see come from, Paquito."

Paquito returns his attention to Mr. Frank and picks the conversation back up. "That also happens to me, Mr. Frank. Do not forget that I also like to paint."

Paquito stands up and walks casually across the living room, trying to approach the little thing in the corner that has caught his attention, but he ends up disappointed; it is just another small framed sketch of the old man. For a moment, he thought it would be a family photograph. He turns a little to the side and looks at one of the old man's paintings. "The little painting in the corner catches my attention. I think it represents some experience of yours, Mr. Frank."

"And what about it grabs your attention, Paquito? It's opaque and cold colors? The image you see of a rich man ignoring a beggar? Or is it that you are so skilled in art that you can distinguish, through the pulse or the brushstrokes on the canvas, the author's feelings?"

"Well, I am a painter of very little experience—I didn't even graduate with anything that has to do with art or painting—but its colors make me wonder. They reflect grief and inspire sadness. But more than anything else, the picture makes me uneasy."

"Well, boy, as you can see, there are two people who meet; one is wealthy and powerful, and the other is a poor devil, a beggar. The rich represent a society—any society with political arrangements and legal or social order; the other represents the other society—that is, the people themselves, not the system or the government. One makes you sad, and the other makes you angry. Am I right?"

Paquito confirms this with a slight smile.

"This is because of the system. Mankind responds to pity. We humans are so strange. We conduct ourselves and react according to circumstances. The man we feel sorry for when he is in the hole is the same man we envy when he possesses what we do not. That is why I do not believe grief or pity is the best option. After all, that pity is an emotion that, if not handled wisely, can yield poor results. That's why the world is shit."

"Well, Mr. Frank, just figure," Paquito says, "how are you not going to feel sorry for a disabled person? I have seen many women in the street, sometimes even carrying children in their arms, naked, under a sun that burns them, or in winter times, you see them out there without even a coat. It is not easy to deny or refrain from pity."

"That is hard, Paquito. You are right." Mr. Frank sits. "Not all circumstances are the same; they differ. This is why I speak at the level of societies as a whole. Some men, I don't know why, always react to the extreme. It's like even if the correct path is clear, an overreaction can provoke a worse situation."

"What do you mean, Mr. Frank?"

"I have seen many times that racism problems occur in communities and towns. For democracy and to avoid further misfortunes, the government and leaders of those communities make laws. They try to meet certain marks and end up making laws that include people because of their race—in a company, for example. This can bring inconveniences to the productive system of the company, and that can affect an entire country."

"But that seems to make sense to me."

"It makes sense for one thing, and for another, not so much. As I told you, they seek to avoid a social mess, but they also end up having to incorporate someone without adequate preparation for a particular job. Do you understand? Just to avoid a lawsuit."

"Mr. Frank, I can tell you that sometimes I have good ideas, but I have to let them go. In the end, I find them unworthy."

"When an idea comes to your head, don't let it go," Mr. Franks says. "As silly as it may seem, let it sprout, find the freedom it needs to flourish, to grow. The important thing is to be born, my dear boy. It is like the fearlessness of a newborn tree; when it is born, no matter where or from what ground it comes out, it is born. Many of them are born beneath irons or obstructed by stones, but like anyone, they always search for the source of life, seeking the light of the sun. I know you've been there."

"That sounds quite philosophical, Mr. Frank." "In similar circumstances, you might see the water stream of a river, Paquito. The water rushes on any ground. They run, and run, and run aground, and pluck their own ways until they create bodies of water running in the same direction." He sneaks a look to see Paquito's reaction.

"I think I understand what you mean, Mr. Frank. But not every idea is good. Some can even make one fail. I have seen that, although I seem to be a person of little experience and only a boy to you. And I think to continue to insist on a bad idea is a bad idea in itself."

"And how can you identify a good idea, Paquito?"

This question surprises the boy, as he prepared no counteroffensive. "Well, by how..." The boy hesitates.

"When you feel confident you can expect a positive result."

"Don't forget what I said of the one tree when it was born. It germinates, but sometimes it finds itself obliged to dodge the obstacles in its way. When you talk about results, it is because you undertake the task of developing an idea your way with specific results in mind. Just because you do not achieve exactly the outcome you wanted, does not mean the idea was a bad one. It's important to warm to the idea that changing things or things not going as you wanted can be beneficial for you. It may hurt at the beginning because your illusion dies, but in the long run, it is for your own good." "Well, I can tell you how very exciting it is to achieve a goal, succeed as expected, and see the fruits of your efforts. It is really great. I think that, despite everything, you have to be realistic. This world moves for money. Having a lot of money gives you more guarantees, in addition to luxuries and comforts." Paquito smiles lightly. "It can't hurt."

"When that's the case, that's fine, *chiquillo*, but what about when it is not? The bigger the illusion, the greater the frustration when it's not achieved. I'm looking very negative, right?" He smirks. "Think about a race and the many athletes who take part in it. At the end of the competition, we only see two or three of them—those who win first place, second place, and maybe third. But what of the other twenty or thirty who participated?"

Mr. Frank walks slowly around the room. He is lost in a gaze out the window, looking for the horizon that stands out through the amber curtains. There is no longer a scathing smile on his lips. Instead, he is stoic. He hears nothing but the mute silence and that graceful sight of nature. "Maybe they end the race with the slight hope of having another chance and better luck next time. Maybe they'll have it, or maybe they won't and will suffer once more a painful failure. And maybe, my friend, after a few failures, they will discover another path that leads to other matters—maybe the same, better, worse, who knows?" He tilts his head and looks at the boy.

"I have to go, Mr. Frank. It was a good conversation. Thanks for the tips. I really appreciate it."

"We humans see what we experience only fleetingly, Paquito. That which we enjoy or suffer passes unnoticed. I don't know if you understand me." Mr. Frank appears entranced, ignoring Paquito's farewell. "At least one of those twenty who lost that race left and abandoned their career. Maybe they did something else, even if they would have done better in the next race. Or maybe they did better at what they did next. Imagine a brute man in the audience who, after the bitter experience of failure, rather giving incentive to continue trying, catches the racer's attention and says, 'Why not go do something else, asshole? You're wasting your time with that shit! You're a failure!'" Mr.

Frank laughs rudely, enjoying the brutality with which he has narrated the hypothesis.

"When you live many years, my young friend, you see so many things that you previously could not see. Many achieve their dreams and come to have all the money in the world. They buy everything they ever wanted, achieve fame, and become leaders—even gods in the eyes of millions of fans around the world, and then...they become suicide statistics. Sometimes, you can understand that some people took their lives because of some kind of problem: they lost a job; they had many debts; they were not loved by the person they were in love with. These are weak people, right? But understand, people who have it all—everything normal people always dream about—have more to lose.

"I have also thought about people who have died or perhaps were injured on a private plane or a luxury sports boat. I think, if they hadn't had a private plane, maybe they'd be alive today— less wealthy perhaps, but alive. But I also think of those others, perhaps many more, who have killed themselves for having nothing, because of hunger. Maybe they were poisoned because they ate something that was already expired. You know, people with little money looking for the cheapest food that a supermarket puts on sale. Many kill themselves by riding in scrap metal—those cars on the road without the appropriate conditions and no security whatsoever." He smiles cautiously. "I'm being fair, right?"

He adds, "So you see, dear big boy, it is personal, and one never knows. As frustrating as it may be, never complain. If you feel like crying, cry, but never complain. There is something positive in each failure, just as there is something negative in each success."

Now Mr. Frank pauses. He remains suspended in his mind, and a few seconds later, he looks to where the boy is.

"Where are you going, boy?" he asks Paquito when he sees him walking to the exit of the house. Paquito looks at him but does not say anything. Mr. Frank looks at his watch, then through the window; it is late enough to go to sleep.

There is too much weight on Paquito's back from the frustrations, discouragements, and disappointments that have occurred in his time on earth. It's another ordinary day, and he stands in front of the window watching the outside world, bored and serene. Then he turns around and sits in front of his canvas. The painting remains unfinished. He begins to brush wildly and imprecisely, relieving himself on the canvas. He loses himself in the colors without even looking for a perfect combination, totally robbed by the disappointment that inspired his work, in the style of van Gogh. He spends this moment giving all his feelings to that piece of cloth.

The ego of the spirit he was born with gave him an oasis of serenity without him even realizing, and now he feels a renewed inspiration for life and faithfully intends to reveal this in his first touches. That restless dreamer type, from so many mundane memories, he now distills a light of candor and an adaptation of a work that was not his own.

And through his window, he sees a little bird—a beautiful cardinal perched on the branch of a leafy tree next to his bedroom. This scene gives light to his soul, and he finds the perfect picture to bring about—one that is real and not an intrusive, absurd, dismantled illusion.

"Where has my imagination gone now?" he reflects. "What am I seeing here?"

He surprises himself by painting with such enthusiasm. "I'm paying attention to a little bird and a tree, and I even like what I see. Where does this inspiration come to me from?"

The boy notices that the work he is doing now has nothing to do with his style. His fears separate from the passion that has always characterized him. He is not interested in moving away from his goal, which is and has always been most important in his aspirations to achieve success in life.

Several years have passed since the last time Paquito saw Mr. Frank, and he closely inspects what is going on in this improvised piece of art, the little bird and tree so similar—almost identical—to the one the elder showed him back then. That same painting his friend, with such wisdom, had used as the basis to lecture him about freedom and love, things that, according to the old man, are really important in life.

"So many things indirectly bring me closer to Mr. Frank," whispers Paquito, enraptured by the painting he's working on. "This is another sign that there must be something special between me and that man. We have the same taste, even though my priorities are not the same as his. But, what could it be? The truth is that I have never pressed the issue."

Paquito remains very thoughtful, then abruptly makes a decision. It is spontaneous, but firm and clear. He abandons the half-finished painting and leaves his room, runs into the hallway, and encounters his mom.

"Hey, boy. What's going on? You're really in a hurry, huh?"

He smiles at Mrs. Rosa but says nothing.

"Hey, boy!" Mrs. Rosa insists, and now more seriously adds, "What is it? Where are you going?" "I'm fine, Mom, but I have to go do something."

His mother's questioning makes him stop and wonder what he should really do in order to quench his curiosity. Then a past conversation with his mom comes flooding back, specifically the part when she mentioned that his father had financed a lot.

"Mom, you told me Dad purchased a lot, right?"

"Yes, he financed a piece of land nearby. Why do you ask?" "Where exactly?"

"You know on the way to the metro station? It would be about five or six blocks away, on Clove Avenue."

Paquito nods as he compares the distances between the apartment where he lives with his mom, Mr. Frank's place, and the land with the old little house that his father once financed.

"There is an open space there," Mrs. Rosa says. "There is not much built there yet, basically just trees and bushes."

Paquito listens to the things his mother tells him, then leaves without saying goodbye, his priorities determined by his curiosity. In the midst of this barrage of thoughts, his mind returns to his friend, one he spent his childhood with, with whom he shared his first attempts of doing business and earning wealth, and with whom once he suffered many failures. It's been a few years since he's seen Aldo, and he decides to take a detour to see him.

He takes a few steps and crosses a couple of corners. He knows it is the right road, but for some reason, he feels shuffled. This strange feeling is inopportune, and he must trust his memories of love, pain, and melancholy. He follows his instinct. He does not want anything to distract from being reunited with Aldo or stop him from sharing his curiosity and revelation with him.

He stands in front of the house where he knows he will find his friend Aldo. Once more, he exhibits an expression of confusion but also smiles. It doesn't matter. He knocks on the door, but nobody answers. He knocks a second time, but nobody opens it. Paquito waits for a few seconds, then notices that someone is moving inside, and finally, the door slowly opens. But it is not the face of his friend that he sees. What he sees is the face of an aged man, surely in his seventies, looking at him intently and smiling. Paquito nervously greets him with a *good afternoon* while trying discreetly to recognize him. Aldo's father is not that old, so Paquito speculates that he could be a grandfather he never knew about.

"Paquito?" the man says.

"Yes, I'm Paquito," Paquito responds, very surprised. He tries again to recognize the man who knows his name, but he is confused. "No. No, I'm sorry. I'm sorry." Then Paquito turns around and leaves hurriedly, like someone who has seen a ghost. As Paquito runs away from the house, the aged man keeps calling him.

"Hey! Where are you going? Hey!"

But Paquito ignores him, believing that he got to the wrong house, and does not look back. The boy advances a couple of corners, then sits on a bench, looking as weary as if he ran a mile.

Paquito eventually gets up and keeps walking. He arrives at the house where he hopes to see his friend Mr. Frank and knocks on the door. Nobody answers. He tries again, and still no one responds. He moves to the window that's next to the main door, and with what little he can see, he does not spot the old man. Paquito grabs and turns the doorknob, then cautiously enters while calling Mr. Frank's name. He calls him a few times, but no one answers. His curiosity forces him to look around for Mr. Frank and then for something that confirms his suspicion about the truth of his friend's identity. In a hurry, he goes through the living room and also the kitchen, but he still doesn't see anything that catches his attention. He moves on and walks toward the door that leads to the patio.

"The grave!"

Without any hesitation, Paquito gets closer, feeling an uncontrollable desperation to see who is buried down in the pile of stones. He's short of breath as he approaches it and takes a big inhale before uncovering the name on the cross; the name is one he least expected.

"Virgil Dauhajre! I can't believe this. How can it be?"

Paquito is embroiled in confusion and again moves around to look for Mr. Frank but fails to find him. He feels sob bubbling up as his mind goes crazy.

"It is my dad's name?" He is dying of surprise.

"Is my dad buried here?" the boy insists. "And what are you doing here?" Paquito asks this without being able to see anyone, but in the air is the cologne Mr. Frank always wears. Still, there is no one else here.

"And you? Who are you?" he fiercely insists without any reply. He is stunned, almost dead. Suddenly, he thinks this is a dream or maybe that he is going crazy. With his hands, Paquito clenches his head.

Then comes that melody the old man always plays—that smooth and perfect piece of music by Paul Mauriat called "Pearl Fishers." Without hesitation, the boy turns around, but it takes great effort. He feels tired and clumsy, suffocated; fear is killing him and curiosity too. Limited by exhaustion, he stands in front of the painting that is covered by the beautiful blanket of fine linen, and in a single swipe, he reveals it.

"No. No, no, no..."

From Paquito's open mouth comes a silent scream straight from the soul that rumbles the house. He can't believe the image he sees. It is inexplicable; it makes no sense. Stunned, he tilts his head slowly, not understanding or believing life or reality. Involuntarily, he backs up and hits a small table behind him, dropping a couple of frames to the floor.

"Damn you, cruel and miserable mind. You couldn't be more hypocritical!"

It is not a painting, but rather a piece of glass—a mirror. And in it is a figure that does not correspond with what Paquito would have expected to see. Now and with all cruelty, he discovers the truth in front of his eyes.

Under a sea of tears, with a sweaty face and careless beard, Paquito suffers this discovery revealed by that damn mirror hanging before him. He learns that his skin is no longer as smooth as he believed it to be and that his vigor is a thing of a past, which he, old and tired, has been denying for so long. But his mind has been strong when he needed it to be, when he wanted to return to who he once was—it was all more than a memory; it was a whole life of fantasies and hallucinations.

Looking at his true and only face, Paquito sadly accepts that he is alone again, that young Paquito was his other reality, his other truth. He settles and lets his body relax, feeling defeated, surrendering. "The mind is strong and makes you live and be where your body cannot."

Again and coldly, he looks in the mirror. He picks from the floor an old framed photograph of him and his mother, Mrs. Rosa, then a second photo of his high school graduation. And then he sees it... Hanging on the wall is the never-finished painting of the little bird; it's been there for so many years.

"When it can't fulfill your imagination, it takes you to sleep. My memory fulfilled my imagination, but that past cannot change. That is why my memory-based hallucinations were the only source of living I looked for, and that happiness forbade me reality."

He is flabbergasted, and his gaze is clueless and cold.

"But which reality?" He nods to himself.

"What is reality, after all? Who would define it?"

He wears a sad smile. "But I've lived, after all."

Don Paquito cries so hard that his tears cascade down his cheeks and his soul collapses into a spring of pure feelings. His chest hurts, but he is not interested in stopping as one who finds immense pleasure in relief and wants to open completely—even die if necessary. But then he smiles. The old man is revived. He stands up and returns to the courtyard. He stops in front of the grave and kneels carefully; his vintages are not few anymore, and sudden movement does not suit him. He takes a piece of towel from the side of the tomb and dusts off the fine black marble cross stuck above the lot of land and discovers a name.

"How much happiness and tranquility it brings me to always have you here with me. Even in silence and covered with this firm land, you've remained as any responsible family member would. How sad it makes me to know the way you left. That is why I always ask the magician of creation; the all-powerful who can do anything; the one who many, many times asks us to both believe and to accuse him of everything—good or bad—as the author of all entirety, to make sure you are where you deserve to be. I never saw or knew you to do anything wrong on this earth, and it hurts me to not have you with me—looking at you and you looking at me; talking to you and you talking to me; listening to you and you hearing me. Everyone has those they go to with their tails between their legs. You were that for me. Those faithful to a higher power have excused your absence, always saying the same thing: 'Thy will be done.'"

He grows tired of kneeling. He stands facing the grave with his teary eyes, looking at the name written on the cross.

He has lived his years between two universes, where in the one, the past is the present and it falters the mind, where the north and the south do not find their way, where the strong cold is suffocated by the indolent sun, where minutes and hours do not define time. The mind is the real world that never perishes.

He hears someone knocking at his door. He's surprised; no one ever knocks on his door, and only in his mind he has had any visits. Slow and curious, he approaches the window that is next to the door and peers through it discreetly. He sees no one. As he turns away, again he hears someone knocking at the door, and again he pauses, then decides to finally open it.

"Hi, Paquito," the man says.

With a sad smile on his lips, he is flooded with gratitude at the sight of Aldo, his childhood friend, the same one he earlier sought but did not recognize while he still wandered in the depths of the most compassionate part of his mind. "Hi, Aldo." Paquito moves aside—a sign for his friend to enter.

"You're good?" Aldo asks with concern. "Yes."

"Well, maybe you don't remember," Aldo says, "but you were at my house just a few minutes ago, and when I opened the door, you ran away."

"Do you think I'm crazy, Aldo?" Paquito asks with shame.

"What are you talking about, brother?" He cracks a smile. "We're all crazy, thanks to God! Just imagine, my friend, old and sane." Aldo laughs aloud. "What would we have left, then? And how would you define craziness, anyway, Franky? Is there any gap between craziness and sanity?"

Loosening up, Paquito smiles too.

"Those who claim to know about human behavior live by finding new modalities and changing the names of mental deficiencies or combining them," Aldo says. "Surely a thesis of today will be questioned tomorrow for a new discovery of an English doctor, because if the professional in question is a graduate from a college in the third world who makes the discovery, either it is a mistake or it is not reliable."

Both men laugh. Even Don Paquito laughs out loud at the almost racist comment Aldo has made.

"But today, my friend, let's break the routine. Let's not think of medicines and healthcare today." Aldo moves to the kitchen and asks Paquito where he keeps the drinks. Paquito tells him, and Aldo opens one of the cabinets and hands him a bottle of whiskey, smiling. He takes a couple of glasses from the counter, then adds ice and some orange juice from the fridge.

"Let's see, old man. Smile at me and let's enjoy this moment to the fullest. There aren't that many left."

And so the friends share in conversation. They remember the old times together, from childhood to sharing and fighting for their dreams of being great, rich, and famous. They also celebrate with melancholy those failures and the many bitter experiences the whole thing brought them.

A few whiskeys down—perhaps a little more than what they should have consumed considering how old they are now—they feel the heavy and tired tongue from so many stories and anecdotes told. Aldo gets up from the chair and walks toward the back of the house. He stops and looks pensively at the grave at the back of Paquito's house.

"Do you remember the day you heard about your dad, Paquito?"

"I remember it very well."

"We were together when Mrs. Rosa called to let you know." Aldo turns to look at Paquito. "Do you remember when you started to fix this old house? I imagine that was the dream your father had—to have a better place for you and for Mrs. Rosa, without expecting anything to happen to him. Then after our business failures, you decided to work more seriously. You worked so hard to collect extra money to put with the money you had from the sale of your and Lucia's house to improve this one. Remember?"

"Yes, I do, Aldo." Paquito frowns. "I don't keep up with it as I should now."

Aldo pays little attention to this comment. "And to think Mrs. Rosa passed away only one year after learning about Mr. Dauhajre's disappearance. At least she had the satisfaction of finding him before she was gone, along with the reassurance that he really was a good man. He never abandoned his family but died in a freak accident. After all that mystery around the way he died… It's a miracle anyone found him in the depths of a river so deep."

Aldo approaches the room again and takes a seat. "Good, Paquito. I'm glad you at least remember that. It is just as important as those selective memories that you keep handy." Aldo laughs for some time about that. Eventually, he pauses, taking a more solemn attitude. "I had a couple of months where I didn't see you, Paquito. I know we are a little distant, but remember that I will always be there. You know you don't have to feel alone, right?"

When Paquito says goodbye to Aldo, he squeezes his hand and hugs him like any brother would. Paquito accompanies him to the door with a sigh of satisfaction and joy.

"See you later, Paquito, and better if you control that mind of yours. It's time to live in reality." "Reality? What's that?"

Paquito cracks a smile and watches his old friend walk away, then closes the door. A soft sound catches his attention. It seems that it is coming from outside. He opens the window next to the main door, and his smile expands. He dazzles as he looks up at the sky and feels a few drops of rain that fall onto his extended hand. He looks straight ahead, directly toward a bushy, leafy tree in front of him, and says, "It seems as if the rain scares you."

THE END

ACKNOWLEDGEMENTS

For the complexion of a book there are things that are basic. Taking the necessary time is vital, but also having the right environment is decisive and, in this sense, the silence and collaboration from those with whom you share your workplace helps a lot.

Having said this, I want to take advantage and thank the assistance of some academic institutions from which ideas and key notes for the book emanated, as well as the more direct collaboration of Bernadette Alvarado; my daughter, by Cristian Alvarado; my son, by Omar Alvarado; my brother, and Marida Aybar; my moral support.

ABOUT THE AUTHOR

J. Marlbor Alvarado was always a quiet and shy child who spends most of his time trying to understand the meaning of life and reality. He was born in Santo Domingo City, in the Dominican Republic on July, 26, 1963, and moved to the United State of America in 1989 where he continued studying languages, and completed a high-college degree in International Affairs at WIU, in Prussia, Pennsylvania, USA. He fell in love with literature and started writing at very young age, from which he has published numerous articles in newspapers, but also the first of his books: 'Dominicanismo Universal' (current affairs), in August of 2001; a source of consultant at: Dept. of Latin America and Caribbean Studies at Duke University, in NC (2005). He also published 'La Sombra del Poder Global y el Terrorismo Internacional' in 2005 (current affairs), and in 2015 published: 'La Sombra del Campo'; which became his first published novel.

In his free time Alvarado enjoys painting and listen his favorite music; jazz.

Alvarado resides in Brooklyn, NY, and is father to his daughter; Bernadette Alvarado, and to his son; Cristian Alvarado.

www.ingramcontent.com/pod-product-compliance
Lightning Source LLC
LaVergne TN
LVHW091008080826
845145LV00003B/1175

* 9 7 8 0 5 7 8 8 7 5 7 7 4 *